"WHAT DRIVES YOU WILL..." nipped the back of her neck playfully.

"Wouldn't you like to know."

"Yes, as a matter of fact, I would. What does it take to find out?"

She faced him. "No way. A girl has to have a few secrets."

"I like mysterious women," he said with a smile.

"What's the smile for?" Annie asked.

"You want me to kiss you, don't you?"

She blushed. "What makes you say that?"

"I can tell. You have that look. You want me."

She laughed, but she could feel the blush spreading. "Oh, I do, do I?"

"It's written all over your pretty little face, Annie."

"Oh, good grief!"

"Admit it, Hartford. You want my body. You've wanted it since you first laid eyes on me. Well, guess what?"

Laughter bubbled out of her. "What?"

"I'm yours, baby."

She felt something in her stomach dip. He turned her around in his arms and gazed down at her face. She tried to look serious, but it was difficult. "I don't want to rush you, Sam."

"Rush me, Annie. Please."

WHAT ARE *LOVESWEPT* ROMANCES?

They are stories of true romance and touching emotion. We believe those two very important ingredients are constants in our highly sensual and very believable stories in the LOVE-SWEPT line. Our goal is to give you, the reader, stories of consistently high quality that may sometimes make you laugh, sometimes make you cry, but are always fresh and creative and contain many delightful surprises within their pages.

Most romance fans read an enormous number of books. Those they truly love, they keep. Others may be traded with friends and soon forgotten. We hope that each LOVESWEPT romance will be a treasure—a "keeper." We will always try to publish

LOVE STORIES YOU'LL NEVER FORGET BY AUTHORS YOU'LL ALWAYS REMEMBER

The Editors

Loveswept ®916

THE LAST SOUTHERN BELLE

CHARLOTTE HUGHES

BANTAM BOOKS
NEW YORK · TORONTO · LONDON · SYDNEY · AUCKLAND

To "The Girls."
I'm a better person
having known you.

THE LAST SOUTHERN BELLE
A Bantam Book / December 1998

ISBN 0-553-44594-4

Published simultaneously in the United States and Canada

*Bantam Books are published by Bantam Books, a division of Bantam Dou-
bleday Dell Publishing Group, Inc. Its trademark, consisting of the words
"Bantam Books" and the portrayal of a rooster, is Registered in U.S.
Patent and Trademark Office and in other countries. Marca Registrada.
Bantam Books, 1540 Broadway, New York, New York 10036.*

PRINTED IN THE UNITED STATES OF AMERICA

OPM   10 9 8 7 6 5 4 3 2 1

PROLOGUE

"Annie, you make a beautiful bride."

Winston Hartford smiled down at his daughter proudly. "In fact, there was only one woman whose beauty surpassed yours, and that was your dear sweet mother, God rest her soul."

"She looks like Cinderella," Vera Holmes, the Hartfords' longtime housekeeper said, giving a girlish sigh. She had raised Annie after the death of her mother, when Annie was just a young girl. The two were as close as any mother and daughter could be. Annie told Vera everything. Well, almost everything. What she didn't tell, the housekeeper usually guessed.

Annie gazed down at the satin creation she wore and shook her head. Her dress resembled the hoop skirts of the Old South, only the designer had forgone the hoop and used a half-dozen crinoline slips instead. The effect was both dramatic and bothersome as hell, as far as Annie was concerned. She suspected there was enough room under her skirt to shelter all the stray cats and dogs in Atlanta.

"I feel more like Cinderella's carriage," she told Vera, although she was hesitant to complain, since the gown had been a gift from her intended's mother. It was a Paris original that had made all other dresses look drab in comparison. No expense had been spared on its making. Annie and her future mother-in-law had flown over twice in the Concorde for Annie's fittings, compliments of Winston Hartford, who not only didn't have the time but wouldn't have had any idea how to go about that sort of thing. The two women had stayed in the best hotel, eaten at four-star restaurants, and replenished Annie's wardrobe, right down to the bare essentials.

Annie suspected she now owned more linen dresses and hats than Nancy Reagan. Obviously, her future mother-in-law had hoped to dissuade her from wearing jeans. Not that Annie had any intention of giving them up. She'd spent much of her childhood in starched pinafores and mary janes, and the private schools she'd attended had required the ugliest uniforms money could buy. Then there was that fancy finishing school where the young ladies were expected to wear dresses, panty hose, and heels at all times. If a student wasn't dressed appropriately, with her hair and makeup just so, she'd better have a darn good explanation. Annie had spent much of her time in the headmistress's office explaining away her casual-clothes preference.

Once she'd graduated, Annie had traded in her demure skirts and blouses for denims and cotton pullovers. Even when she was expected to entertain, she didn't go overboard. Her makeup needs had been reduced to mascara, a light dusting of blush, and one swipe with her tube of lipstick. Luckily, she could get away with it. At twenty-nine, her skin was still youthful and flawless, and she had no desire to go clogging up her pores with a bunch of gunk. Today was different; however. She'd spent more than an hour with a professional makeup artist, and the woman who looked back at her from the mirror now only vaguely resembled the old Annie. Her shoulder-length blond hair had been pinned back so tightly that her eyes appeared slanted. An elaborate veil sat atop her head. She wondered why one wedding required so much pomp and fuss. Had it been up to her, she would have insisted on something simple.

Annie realized Vera and her father were staring at her. Probably wondering why she wasn't kicking her heels in absolute joy over the fact that she was marrying the most eligible bachelor in all of Atlanta. Eldon Wentworth was not only movie-star handsome with his blond hair and fashionable clothes, he was smooth and polished and could charm his way into any woman's heart. Except hers. Annie liked him fine as a friend, but the thought of sharing an intimate relationship with the man left her cold.

Her father stepped back and viewed his daughter from another angle. The room had been filled with bridesmaids and a fussy flower girl only moments before. They'd scattered like chickens the moment Winston Hartford had knocked on the door. Annie was used to this reaction. She'd learned long ago that most people were intimidated by the man. "Daddy, what are you doing?" she asked, feeling somewhat embarrassed at the way he was looking at her.

"I want to remember exactly how you look on this day," he said. "I will carry the memory with me always."

She blushed. Her father was not the sentimental type, but he was obviously making an exception today. "Both of you look quite elegant as well," Annie said, forcing a smile she didn't feel. The tension in the room was thick enough to chew. If her father suspected she wasn't blissfully happy over her upcoming marriage, he didn't say anything. Not that he would. He had handpicked Eldon Wentworth and was looking forward to the union.

"You've made me the happiest man alive," he said, as though reading her mind. "You don't know how badly I've wanted to see you married into a good family."

Oh, yes she did, Annie thought. She had been raised and schooled to marry well.

". . . and the Wentworths are one of the oldest and most respected families in Atlanta."

Annie wished she had a dime for every time she'd heard those words come out of her father's mouth during the past six months.

"Eldon will take good care of you. He loves you very much, you know."

Annie wondered why her father felt she needed someone to take care of her. Did he think she was utterly helpless? As far as Eldon loving her, she suspected the only person Eldon loved was himself. That would explain why he was always looking in the mirror. If he was dressed impeccably, it was because he fussed with himself all the time. Lately, he'd begun to fuss with her as well. If she so much as spilled a drop of something on her clothes, he went straight for a cloth and the club soda and insisted on rubbing the spot out himself. He watched her constantly when they went out to dinner, afraid she would spill something in her lap. Annie enjoyed tormenting him by ordering soups and messy pasta dishes. Served him right for being so persnickety.

And this business of Eldon being in love with her. Oh, sure, he was showering her with attention now, but that would change in time. His family might be well respected, but hers was one of the richest and most powerful. The fact that her father owned several Fortune 500 companies only sweetened the pot. Eldon liked money and power. He had already been put in charge of her father's various holdings, and the marriage would secure a place for him once Winston Hartford was forced to retire. Eldon had played his cards right where her father was concerned, and now he would reap the rewards. What saddened Annie more than anything was that her father had not been able to see through the ruse. Or perhaps he hadn't wanted to. For the first time in his life Winston Hartford had let his emotions rule his decision. He saw Eldon Wentworth as the son he'd lost years before and nobody was going to make him see differently.

Annie listened absently as her father continued to sing her future husband's praises. She gazed out the side window, where the family's white stretch limousine waited to whisk the couple away once they'd exchanged their vows. They would be taken to Atlanta's finest country club, where they and their eight hundred guests would dine on lobster flown in from Maine the night before.

Her father had insisted on choosing the menu as well as the church, one large enough to accommodate a sizable guest list, many of whom were celebrities and dignitaries. There would be no slouches at his daughter's wedding, Winston had exclaimed. Annie had gone along with his suggestions, simply because she'd had no desire to join in the planning of what was being touted as the wedding of the year. Television crews and newspaper photographers had been in place since the wee hours of the morning. They would no doubt follow the couple to the airport, where they'd take off for a month-long honeymoon in Europe. Annie dreaded it, and she continued to hope that something would happen so she wouldn't have to go through with it.

Now, as the time grew near, she knew she would not be rescued. Before, there had been numerous parties to take her mind off her problems. It seemed everybody in Atlanta was anxious to throw open their doors in celebration of the upcoming marriage. And what of the bridal showers? There'd been one for lingerie, another for kitchen items, and yet another for linens and bath accessories. And just in case an item had been overlooked, someone had held a miscellaneous shower. If that weren't enough, she and Eldon had attended two showers where other couples had presented them with tools. Tools? She wasn't sure Eldon even knew what to do with such things. The last shower, also with couples, was given to stock the wet bar in their new home.

Annie was wasting her time feeling sorry for herself. There would be no white knight rushing in at the last minute to save her. White knights and Prince Charmings were the stuff of fairy tales. They hadn't come around when she was a little girl watching her mother die from a lengthy illness, nor had they shown up when her brother had died in an automobile accident. These were the harsh realities of life, and it didn't matter how much money one had. The only difference was, rich people often had to grieve publicly.

Annie knew she would do as her father expected, simply because she always had. She would marry Eldon and be the perfect wife in her perfect linen dress with matching shoes, and she would bear him perfect children. Eldon claimed that in time she would learn to love him. Annie figured the best she could do was learn to tolerate him.

"Oh, look at the time," her father said, checking his diamond-studded watch. "I'd better get out front so I can personally welcome the governor when he arrives." He leaned forward and kissed his daughter on the cheek. "I wish your mother and your brother were here to witness this," he said. "They would both be very proud."

Annie suspected Bradley would have bopped her one over the head for agreeing to marry Eldon in the first place.

"You take good care of my girl, Vera," Winston said in a voice that commanded respect. "I'll tap on the door when it's time." He hurried out.

"Please lock it," Annie told the woman. "I don't think I can tolerate another gushing bridesmaid."

Vera did as she was asked, then folded her arms over her breasts. "Now that you've decided to go along with this ceremony, the least you can do is smile. You look like you're on your way to a funeral instead of your own wedding."

Annie refused to meet the housekeeper's gaze in the ornately framed mirror. The last thing she needed to do was cry and have her mascara run down her face. "I'm okay," she said, sounding more confident than she felt.

Vera stepped closer. "It's not too late to call it off, Annie," she whispered.

Annie gave a snort. "Oh, yeah? And who's going to eat eight hundred lobster dinners?"

"I hardly doubt that's going to make a dent in your father's bank account, my dear."

"What about the governor? And Daddy? I'll humiliate him in front of all his friends."

"The governor will get over it, and this is not the first time the Hartford family will have faced a scandal."

Annie knew it was true. There had been rumors that her brother had been on drugs or alcohol when he'd lost control of his car on the interstate, killing himself and his best friend. But an autopsy had proved otherwise, and another motorist had come forward stating that Bradley had swerved off the road to keep from hitting a deer.

Vera touched Annie's cheek. "I don't know why you let things go this far, Annie Hartford. You don't love Eldon any more than I do, and I can't stand his loudmouth mother with those big horse teeth of hers. This isn't going to bring your brother back, you know," she added softly.

Annie snapped her head up. "What's that supposed to mean?"

"The one reason you're marrying Eldon Wentworth to begin with is because your father likes him so much. For some odd reason, Eldon reminds him of Bradley. I don't see the resemblance, personally. Bradley was kind and loving and considerate. Eldon thinks only of himself, and his pocketbook."

"Vera, why did you wait until now to say something? Why didn't you speak up sooner? At least I would have felt I had an ally in this."

"You're almost thirty years old, missy. I'd hoped you would see what a mistake you were making in agreeing to marry a man you don't love."

"What else am I supposed to do? I have no skills."

"You're rich. You'll never have to work a day in your life if you don't want to."

"Everybody needs to have some kind of purpose in life, Vera. As for being rich, I'll probably lose my inheritance if I don't marry Eldon. So I'll need some kind of job."

Vera planted her hands on her hips. "Hard work has never bothered you before, Annie Hartford. I've seen you work yourself silly in soup kitchens and homeless shelters, and there's not another woman in this town who can organize a fund-raiser the way you can. Good Lord, girl, you underestimate your own abilities. But that's because you're overwhelmed with all these other responsibilities."

Annie sighed and fixed her gaze on the window once more. "Well, you're right about one thing, Vera. I don't love Eldon, and I never will. But—" She paused and blinked back tears. "I so wanted to see Daddy happy again. The light seemed to go right out of him when Bradley died."

"People are responsible for their own happiness, Annie," Vera said. "You can't spend the rest of your life pleasing your father. He's the reason you didn't attend the college of your choice, the reason you've never had a place of your own."

"He needs me. Who else is going to plan his dinner parties and take care of his social obligations and make sure he eats right and gets plenty of exercise?"

"He can afford to hire a social secretary and a fitness trainer. In the meantime you could be out making a life for yourself." Vera put her hand on Annie's shoulder. "Don't you think you've done enough, sweetie? You've given up ten years of your life, seeing to his every need, trying to make him happy. Must you marry a man you don't love as well?"

Annie could feel her throat tightening up as she continued to stare out the window. She saw her father's chauffeur jump from the limo and race inside as though something were the matter. "What's wrong with Sneddley?" she asked Vera.

Vera glanced out the window as well. "Oh, he has prostate trouble, the poor man. Runs to the men's room every fifteen minutes. I've nagged him until I'm blue in the face about going to the doctor, but you know how some men are about that sort of thing."

Annie had a sudden thought. It was sheer lunacy, of course, and it would never work, but it was her only hope. "Where does that door lead, Vera?" she asked, motioning to a solid oak door on the opposite side of the room.

"It leads to a hallway that surrounds the church. Toward the back are offices," Vera said.

"Is there a door leading out?"

"Yes, why?"

Annie stood. "Does Sneddley ever leave the keys in the limo?"

"I've no idea. But he keeps an extra set in the glove compartment." Vera frowned. "What are you thinking?"

"I'm taking your advice," she said, giving the woman a kiss on the cheek. "All I've done since Bradley died is try to make up for his absence. I'm tired of trying to make other people happy all the time. I have to think of myself once in a while."

"Good for you," Vera said. "But wait. Aren't you going to tell your father?"

"There's no time." Her eyes misted. "I love you, Vera. When Sneddley comes out of the bathroom, would you try to detain him for a few minutes? Tell him I've disappeared. Ask him to help you search the offices in back. I'll need time to get away."

"Your father is going to knock on that door any minute now. It would be best if you explained to him—"

"I've no time to waste. I only hope I can outrun the photographers."

"Let's go," a resigned Vera said.

Annie threw open the door and raced out, then followed the hall to a door that opened into a courtyard. The limo was less than twenty feet away. Once again, she thought of all the stories she'd read as a child—the knight in shining armor, Prince Charming and his kiss. So many times she'd wished such a figure would show up, pull her onto his horse, and ride to where nothing bad could ever happen to her again.

Utter nonsense.

She was responsible for saving herself.

Annie gathered her skirts and ran.

ONE

"Gin."

Darla Mae Jenkins made a production of discarding her playing card and laying the others out so that they resembled a fan. She pointed a finger at her boss, Sam Ballard. Her nails had been painted the same unusual red color as her hair. Darla swore it was natural, that her family tree was slam full of redheads. But more than one person in Pinckney, Georgia, had seen her sneaking into the back door of the Clip Joint Beauty Salon on Monday morning, when the salon was supposed to be closed. "You owe me thirty-five cents," she told the man sitting across from her, in a drawl that was as thick as sap oozing from a tree.

Sam gave a snort of disgust and studied her cards carefully. Darla had been known to cheat on more than one occasion, and he wasn't about to be taken in by the unscrupulous cardsharp. "You know what I think, Darla Mae? I think you've tucked a few aces in that fancy new garter belt you bought in Athens last week."

Darla stood and mussed his hair, something he hated but tolerated, since they went way back. "Why, Sam Ballard, I can't believe you're accusing me of cheating. You know darn good and well I'm as honest as a barn is broad." She suddenly propped her hands on her hips and regarded him, her hazel eyes clouded with suspicion. "And how, pray tell, do *you* happen to know about my new garter belt? Last time I offered you a peek at what was under my skirts, you turned me down flat."

He remembered well, mainly because she wouldn't let him forget. The incident had occurred in high school, when Darla had ended up in his car after the Sadie Hawkins Day dance. Back then she'd been voted the Girl Most Likely in the school locker room. Sam had known it was a bad idea to go parking out by Woods Lake, but Darla wouldn't take no for an answer. Nevertheless, Sam had drawn the line when she'd climbed into the backseat of his old Ford Fairlane and asked him to join her. He'd done a song and dance about how they were good friends and how much he respected her and so on, but she had seen it as an outright rejection and had been yammering about it ever since.

"Sam, I asked you a question," Darla said. "How did you hear about my new garter belt?"

Sam grinned. "It's a small town, honey. Word gets around. Also heard that you paid a pretty penny for it."

Darla stood and smoothed the wrinkles out of her uniform. Sam complained constantly that her skirt was too tight and too short, but Darla claimed it helped her tips, so he let it go. Besides, Darla did what Darla wanted, and nobody could tell her otherwise. "You're right about the gossips in this town. If I had a nickel for every one of 'em, I wouldn't be waiting tables for a living. A girl can't so much as take a leak without everybody and their mother knowing it."

"Perhaps you should try to be a little more discreet, Miss Jenkins."

"What are you talking about? I'm the queen of discretion."

"Which explains the eighteen-wheeler parked in front of your mobile home last weekend."

She waved off the remark. "Oh, that was just an uncle visiting."

"How many uncles you got, Darla, honey?"

"Don't get smart with me, Sam, or you'll be looking for a new waitress." She glanced out the front window of the Dixieland Café as she spoke. "Great balls of fire! Would'ja get a load of that?"

Sam swiveled around on the red vinyl counter stool and gave a low whistle at the sight of the white stretch limo sitting in the middle of Main Street. "Well, now. I wasn't aware of any dignitaries visiting Pinckney. Must be here for the Okra Festival." He'd barely gotten the words out of his mouth before he noticed smoke seeping out from beneath the hood. "Uh-oh, looks like trouble in Tinseltown. I'd better go see."

"What d'you mean, you'd better go see? You ain't no mechanic, Sam. Hey, wait for me," Darla said, forgetting her customers for the time being and following him out of the restaurant.

A number of people had already gathered on the sidewalk, including Mott Henry, the town drunk. From the looks of it, he hadn't shaved or bathed in days. He watched the excitement for a moment, then turned and moseyed down the sidewalk toward the liquor store, obviously more interested in buying his next bottle than in the commotion in the street. The Petrie sisters, still spry in their eighties, stood at the edge of the crowd, each holding a brown sack from Odom's Grocery. They craned their necks to see over a group of teenage boys.

"Is anyone in there?" a man in the crowd called out. "You can't see diddly with them tinted windows."

"I can't figure it," Darla said. "Why would anybody put tinted windows in a danged limo? Shoot, if I was riding in one of those suckers, I'd want all my friends to be able to see."

Sam was amused by the town's response to the limo. One would have thought a flying saucer had just landed on Main Street, and everybody was waiting for the hatch to open and a whole slew of aliens to walk out. It just proved the town needed more in the way of entertainment.

Bic Fenwick, the town mechanic, happened by at that moment in his tow truck. On the door of his truck someone unskilled had painted THE CAR DOCTOR. He parked along the side of the street and hurried over, looking puffed up with importance. He knocked on the driver's window. "Hey there, did you know you got smoke comin' out from under your hood?"

Sam chuckled. "I'd say it was a given, Bic."

"Well, you never know what people can see with them tinted windows," Bic said. He pressed his face against the window and squinted. "You want me to take a gander at what's under your hood?" he shouted, as if the tinted windows might interfere with the person's hearing as well. Sam figured whoever was in the limo was getting a good laugh.

The window whispered down a couple of inches. Sam joined Bic and caught sight of a pair of emerald-green eyes. The woman inside wore a wide-eyed expression that seemed to plead for friendship. At the same time she looked utterly hopeless. Her disheveled hair was the color of ripened wheat, tendrils curled about her face as though caressing her cheeks.

Sam leaned forward. "Look, lady, you can't leave this thing sitting in the middle of the road," he said. "You're blocking traffic. Not to mention my dinner customers. I suggest you get it out of here pronto."

Annie couldn't hide her annoyance. Did the man think she was daft, for Pete's sake? She knew she was blocking traffic, but there wasn't a darn thing she could do about it. "Thanks for your input, Bubba," she said, "but as you can see, I don't have much choice in the matter."

Those standing nearby fell into fits of laughter, including Bic, who slapped Sam on the back. "I guess she put you in your place, *Bubba*."

Sam didn't think it was a damn bit funny. He frowned. "Hey, wait just a minute. Who do you think you're calling—"

Bic cut him off. "Excuse me, miss, do you see a hood release in there?" he asked. "Look to your left, it's about knee-high." He glanced at Sam and rolled his eyes. "Least it is in most cars. No telling where they put 'em in these big suckers."

"Probably next to the wet bar and Jacuzzi," Sam muttered, still stinging from her retort. She might have the prettiest eyes he'd ever seen, but she had a mouth on her that would send most men on their way in a hurry.

There was a metallic click, and the mechanic hurried around to the front of the car. He opened the hood and smoke billowed out. "Jeez, Louise!" Bic exclaimed, backing away from the vehicle. "Looks like it's gonna blow."

"What's going on here?" a voice said.

Sam looked up to find Harry Hester, the sheriff, standing there. He was so bald that most folks called him Kojak behind his back. "This lady's limo is putting out more smoke than a house fire, Harry. She won't even get out of the car. And let me warn you ahead of time," he added. "She's a mouthy little thing."

"Oh, yeah? We'll see about that."

Sixty-year-old Marge Dix elbowed her way through the crowd. Most considered her a sourpuss. "Would you just look at that?" she said, her voice bristling with indignation. "Here we have starving people in this world, and we got folks driving around in cars the size of mobile homes. I hope whoever it is doesn't plan on settling in Pinckney. I just can't abide such vulgarity. Makes me ill, that's what it does."

"Then I wouldn't look if I were you, Marge," Darla told her. "If something made me that sick, I'd march right home, lock the doors, and pull the shades."

Marge regarded Darla. "The Bible says we should store our treasures in heaven."

"Some of us don't want to wait that long for nice things," the waitress replied.

Sheriff Hester stepped closer to the window. "Young lady, I need to see your driver's license," he said. "And I don't want no lip from you. This is a law-abiding town, and the sooner you get used to that fact the better." He glanced at Sam and winked.

"You go, Kojak," Darla said.

Hester shot her a dark look. "Watch it, Darla Mae, or I'll write you a ticket for having an eighteen-wheeler parked in your front yard last weekend."

Inside the limo, Annie Hartford sighed heavily, wishing she could just turn back the clock, to the moment she decided to scramble from the church and hijack her father's limo. It would have been easier marrying Eldon than sitting there with the whole town gawking at her as though she'd just escaped the loony bin. She wished she could disappear into thin air like some cartoon character; instead, it looked like she was going to suffer her share of humiliation.

"I'm sorry, Sheriff, but I don't have my license with me." She waited, knowing he would derive a great deal of pleasure from that fact.

"Oh, really?" He looked about the crowd. "Seems these rich folks don't have to follow the same rules as the rest of us."

"Driving without a license carries a stiff fine, doesn't it, Harry?" Sam said, and saw the green eyes flash at him like summer lightning. Their gazes locked. She seemed to be mentally assessing him, and from the looks of it, she wasn't impressed.

"A fine?" Harry asked. "Oh, yes," he said. "Not to mention possible jail time." A smile twitched the corners of his lips. He was obviously enjoying himself. "She'd better show me a registration for that thing, or there'll be a hanging in the courthouse square." Several in the crowd chuckled.

Darla threw up her hands. "I don't believe what I'm hearing. You are probably scaring the poor woman to death, Harry. Do you know how unprofessional you sound?"

Annie shook her head sadly. Harry and Sam were obviously having a grand ol' time at her expense. "Then get your rope ready, Barney Fife, because I don't have the registration either."

Darla laughed out loud. "You go, girl!"

The sheriff colored fiercely. He leaned closer to the window. "Sam's right about you having a mouth. I don't take kindly to strangers coming into my town and creating a public display, and I sure as heck don't appreciate the lack of respect you're showing me. It's my job to protect the citizens of this fine town."

"And you see me as a possible threat to the citizens?" Annie asked, completely bewildered by his attitude.

His jaw tensed. "I believe we were discussing your lack of respect for authority, missy."

Annie was growing weary of it all. "I have the utmost respect for law officials," she said, "but I will not permit you and your sidekick to publicly ridicule me. Now, I've made it plain I have neither a license nor registration. So you can lock me up or have me shot, but I'd like to speak to my attorney first, because I have every intention of filing a lawsuit against you for your barbarous behavior."

"That's tellin' him, honey," Darla said. "I'll be your witness."

"What'd I ever do to you?" Hester asked Darla. When she didn't answer, he shrugged his shoulders a bit, but his demeanor was no longer intimidating. "Look, lady. How'm I supposed to know this automobile belongs to you?"

"You could use sodium pentothol on her," Sam suggested.

Annie didn't hesitate. "This vehicle doesn't belong to me. I borrowed it."

"You *borrowed* it?" Hester shoved his cap back on his head and scratched his bald spot. He looked at Sam. "She *borrowed* it."

"Yeah, I heard."

Harry hooked his thumbs inside his belt. "I'm afraid I'm going to have to ask you to step out of the car," he said politely. Annie's threat of a lawsuit had obviously worked.

Annie paled at the thought. She would be the laughingstock of the town for sure. And the man they called Sam would be laughing over it until he was old. "I'm afraid that's going to be quite difficult," she said.

The sheriff looked surprised. "Are you handicapped in some way? Do I need to send for a wheelchair?"

"No, nothing like that. It's just—"

"Then, please remove yourself from the vehicle," he said.

Giving an enormous sigh, Annie hit the automatic door unlock and reached for the handle. The sheriff stepped back as she opened the door and tried to extricate herself from the front seat of the limousine. Her cheeks flamed a bright red as the crowd stared in disbelief. The woman in the waitress uniform hurried over and tried to help her. Annie longed to crawl beneath a large rock and never come out.

Sam watched the blonde climb out of the car, taking with her what looked to be hundreds of yards of white satin and lace that made up the most elaborate bridal gown he'd ever laid eyes on. She still wore her veil, even though it had been thrown back haphazardly and now hung askew. Seeing her face in the light was almost humbling. Her facial bones were delicate and very feminine, her skin flawless and glowing with pale peach undertones. Her mouth was full and kissable and probably the sexiest thing he'd ever laid eyes on. He couldn't help but stare openly.

"Jeez, Louise, would you get a load of that?" Bic whispered. "She looks like Glenda, the good witch. How you reckon she managed to get all that there dress in the car with her?"

Sam shook his head. Had he been a betting man, he would have wagered against that possibility. "Beats me."

"Well, now," Sheriff Hester said, clearing his throat loudly. "I don't think I've ever seen anything like this before. Are you supposed to be somewhere, miss? I can run you over in my patrol car. Maybe," he added as he took in the width and breadth of her gown.

"I don't have anywhere I'm supposed to be," Annie said. "I've already been and gone."

"Honey, that dress is to die for," Darla said. "I'll bet you didn't order that from the Sears catalog."

"It came from Paris," Annie said.

"Paris, huh? Fancy that. That's where I do all my shopping. And you make an absolutely beautiful bride." Darla shivered. "Why, I plum get goose chills just looking at you. Sam, ain't she the most gorgeous thing you ever seen?"

Sam had to admit the bride was a sight to behold. From the waist up, the gown was formfitting, revealing ample breasts and a trim waist. From there it flared like a bell and stopped just above her toes, which were encased in satin heels. The woman glanced at him and caught him staring. Sam felt foolish. "Only two things missing as far as I can tell," he said. "The groom and the church."

Darla glared at him. "Samuel Aaron Ballard, that was downright rude!"

Annie met his gaze once again and wondered why a perfect stranger felt compelled to embarrass her further in front of the crowd. "Yes, it was."

"Don't listen to ol' Sam," Darla told her. "Last time he saw a bride, she was running fast as she could in the opposite direction."

Sam glared at her. "Thank you, Darla, for airing my dirty laundry on Main Street," he said tersely.

"Would you two stop fussing long enough for me to do my job?" Sheriff Hester demanded. "Besides, I think it's time we gave Sam a rest about his fiancée running out on him. After all, that was ten years ago."

A sudden smile curved Annie's lips, and two dimples appeared. Sam felt as though a rug had just been pulled out from under him, and he was so discomfited, he threw up his hands. "I don't believe this. One would think nothing of significance has happened in this town since I got jilted."

"The only reason folks remember it so well is 'cause they lost money," Marge Dix said. "That's what they get for betting their earnings."

Sam looked confused. "Marge, what are you talking about?"

"Why don't we go inside the Dixieland Café," Darla suggested quickly. "There's a bit of chill in the air tonight."

"Not till Marge explains herself," Sam said.

Marge looked impatient. "Oh, Sam, how could you not know? Everybody in town had money riding on whether or not you'd be able to convince that little slut to go through with the wedding."

"Slut?" he said.

"I guess there's a lot you didn't know," Marge replied haughtily.

He swung his head in Darla's direction. "Did you know about this bet?"

Darla refused to meet his gaze. "I didn't want to bet, Sam, but the odds against her coming back to you were good, and I needed the money. And, yes, she definitely was a slut, Sam, honey, although I would never have told you had Marge not flapped her big jaws." She tossed Marge Dix a dirty look and went on. "I scratched the little hussy's name off more bathroom walls and phone booths than you could shake a stick at."

"I can't believe you bet *against* me?" he said.

"That was ten years ago," she reminded him. "Can we go inside now?"

"Hold on just a danged minute," Sheriff Hester said. "She can't leave this thing sittin' in the middle of the road. And I still haven't established her identity and who this here vehicle belongs to."

"My name is Katherine Anne Hartford," Annie said, "but my friends call me Annie." She offered her hand.

The sheriff looked flustered. He wiped his right palm on his pants leg and shook her hand. "Pleased to meet you, miss. Now, about that car—"

"It belongs to my father, Sheriff. I was to be married early this afternoon. I changed my mind at the last minute, sneaked out of the church, and took off in this limousine. The keys were in the ignition. The driver was in the men's room at the time. He has prostate trouble and—"

"Never mind all that," Hester said. "Does your father know you have his limo?"

"I have every confidence he does."

"Excuse me, Sheriff," Bic Fenwick said. "May I speak to the lady one second?"

Hester looked greatly annoyed with the interruption. "Is it important, Bic?"

"Concerns her car."

"Is it bad?" Annie asked.

"I'm afraid you done blowed a head gasket, miss," he said, eyeballing her as though she might float away at any moment. "The part don't cost all that much, but I'll have to take the head off the engine. I usually charge five bills for that, but for you—" He leaned closer and winked. "I'll do it at a much better price."

"I'm afraid I don't have any money with me at the moment," Annie said.

He didn't look the least bit bothered by that fact. "That's okay. I can go ahead and tow it over to my garage, and we can discuss payment when you're ready. And under less stressful circumstances, I hope," he added, tossing a dark look at the sheriff. He smiled at Annie. "I just want you to know that some folks in this town are real friendly. You'll just have to overlook the rude ones." He gave Harry another look and walked away.

Annie faced the sheriff squarely. "If you're planning to lock me up for car theft, then go ahead and let's get it over with. After the day I've had, nothing would faze me." She held out her wrists. "You might as well handcuff me while you're at it, although I'm not in the position to run in this garb."

"Now, miss, I was just having a little fun with you," Hester said, obviously stung by Bic's remark.

"Toss me in a cell and throw away the key, for all I care. Frankly, I look forward to a little peace and quiet."

Sam noted the single tear that slid down her cheek. He wondered if it was genuine. "Look," he said. "Harry's not going to throw you in jail. You can't really steal something that already belongs to you."

"What?" Hester regarded him.

"You say it's your father's limo, right?" When Annie nodded, he went on. "If something should happen to your old man, who stands to inherit his estate?"

"I do," she said. "I'm his only heir."

"And that estate would include all motor vehicles?"

Annie could see where he was going with it. "Yes, everything."

"There you go." He looked at Harry. "She can't steal what's already hers."

Hester didn't look convinced. "That sounds real good Sam, but her father ain't dead yet." He glanced at Annie. "Is he?"

"No, sir."

Sam looked at Annie. "I presume you reside with your father."

"That's correct."

"And you're listed as a second driver on his car insurance?"

"Yes."

"And you intend to return the car in a timely fashion, am I right?"

"Well, of course."

"See that, Harry? The young lady is just borrowing the family car." Sam looked pleased with himself. "You can't arrest her for that. Unless you want to end up looking like the bad guy," he added quietly so no one else would hear. Sam didn't know why he was going to bat for the woman; after all, she was a complete stranger, and she had made some disparaging remarks about him. He knew Harry wouldn't lock her up. But he figured as long as he had an audience, he might as well do some fancy lawyer work and drum up a little business.

He reached into his shirt pocket for his business cards and began passing them out. "And I shouldn't have to remind you folks where to come for a good used car. And if you buy your vehicle from me, I'll do you up your last will and testament for half price."

Annie looked confused. "Are you an attorney or a car salesman?"

"Both," he said proudly. He handed her his card. "Here you go. You just might need my services while you're here."

"He damn sure better *not* arrest her," Darla said. "If she goes to jail, I go with her."

Agnes Moore, the town librarian, joined in. "That

goes for me too. And don't think for one minute I won't notify the Friends of the Library and ask for their support."

The Petrie sisters stepped forth, almost shyly. "You can count us in," Edyth Petrie said. Sister Ethyl nodded vigorously.

"Enough already!" Harry all but shouted. "I'm not going to arrest her, but I don't want to hear any belly-aching if she decides to take off in one of your pickup trucks."

"I'll take full responsibility for Miss Hartford," Darla said, slinging her arm around Annie's shoulders. "She can stay at my place while she's here. And she won't have to steal no car 'cause she can use mine anytime she likes."

"Not without a driver's license," Hester reminded her.

Darla stuck her tongue out at him, then smiled at Annie. "Okay, it's all settled. You can stay at my place for as long as you like." She fished a set of keys out of her pocket. "Sam, you'll need to drive her out to my place so she can change clothes. Lord knows she can't be running around dressed like that."

"Me?" Sam looked surprised. "Why should I drive her out to your place?"

Darla sighed her impatience. "Because the dinner crowd is going to start soon, and I'm the only waitress you got working the second shift at the moment. Of course, I'll be glad to let *you* wait on the customers while *I* drive her out."

"Never mind," he grumbled.

Darla looked at Annie. "I think we're close to the

same size. Help yourself to anything in my closet. Sam can drive you back afterward, and I'll whip you up something to eat."

"Thank you for seeing to my itinerary," Sam said, annoyed that Darla had assigned him a list of chores without discussing it with him first.

"You're too kind," Annie told Darla, feeling close to tears. "I have nothing of value to give in return for your hospitality. Except my dress," she said.

Darla's eyes almost popped right out of their sockets. "Your wedding gown? Why, honey, I couldn't possibly accept something like that. I mean, it must've cost a fortune."

"It did," Annie said. "But if you want it, it's yours. I have no use for it."

"Forget it," Sam said. "No minister would ever let Darla Jenkins walk down the aisle in a white wedding dress." Several people who remained in the crowd laughed.

"Bite me, Sam Ballard," Darla said.

Annie noted the humorous light that passed between them and suspected they were only exchanging a little good-natured ribbing. They were obviously close friends, perhaps even lovers. Darla was certainly attractive enough, with her deep red hair and perfect figure. She was on the skinny side, though Annie doubted the woman had ever done a sit-up or attended an aerobics class in her life.

"Besides," Darla was saying, "women wear white all the time these days. Even those who've already been married once."

"That's right," Annie said.

"Even those who've been around the block more times than most mail trucks?" Sam asked.

"Very funny, Sam."

"Perhaps we should inquire as to what color Mr. Ballard's *next* fiancée will be wearing at the wedding," Annie said, unable to resist joining in on the teasing. After all, he'd spared her no mercy. "My guess would be gunmetal gray, to match her leg irons."

Darla burst into laughter, as did several others nearby, including the sheriff. "So she can't get away," she managed as she doubled over with laughter.

Sam crossed his arms over his chest. "Enjoying yourselves, ladies?" His own smile was tight. "If you ever see me walk down the aisle of a church, it'll be because some girl's daddy is holding a shotgun to my back. And since I'm, too, uh, sophisticated to let something like that happen, I don't ever plan to let some woman lead me to the altar with a noose around my neck."

"You have a very romantic way of looking at love and commitment," Annie said.

He arched one dark brow. "You should talk, honey. I'm not the one who stole my daddy's limo and high-tailed it out of town so I wouldn't have to get married."

"Okay, let's break it up." Sheriff Hester waved his arms. "I've got work to do, and I ain't got time to stand around yammerin' all day." He looked at Annie. "I ain't finished with you yet. I want to think on this some more. Don't go leaving town on me, y'hear?"

"Yes, sir." Annie gave a respectful nod.

The crowd thinned. Darla pressed a key into Annie's palm. "Just make yourself at home, honey," she said, and hurried inside the restaurant.

"My Jeep's across the street," Sam told Annie. "Might be easier if I bring it here so you don't have to go traipsing across Main Street dressed like that."

"I'd appreciate it," Annie told him. Once he left her, though, she felt ridiculous standing there while strangers eyed her, wondering whether she was playing with a full deck. Bic Fenwick and what looked to be an assistant mechanic pulled up in a tow truck, and the two went about hooking cables beneath the limo. Annie prayed they wouldn't scratch it. Finally, Sam pulled up in a black Jeep Cherokee. He parked along the side of the road and motioned for Annie to get in. But when she opened the door, she wondered how she would fit into the passenger's seat with all that satin and crinoline. She still couldn't believe she'd managed to get inside the limo, but she'd been desperate to escape at the time. Funny thing about an adrenaline rush—one could sometimes accomplish the impossible. "This isn't going to work," she told Sam.

Bic grinned and winked at her. "Looks like we might have to strap you to the hood of his Jeep," he said. "I got plenty of rope if you need it."

Annie knew the man was just teasing her. "No thanks. I've already entertained this town enough for one day."

Sam climbed out of the driver's side wearing a scowl. He was clearly impatient to be done with the chore Darla had given him. "Is there any way to get that damn train off, or is it attached to the dress?"

"It comes off," she said quickly, wondering why she hadn't thought of that.

"Turn around." Sam searched through several layers of satin before he found what he was looking for, at least two dozen hooks sewn to the train and fastened to threads sewn in the waist of the gown. "Oh, for Pete's sake," he muttered as he worked to pull them free. "I don't know why you women go through all this fuss for a ceremony that only lasts twenty minutes."

Annie could hear the exasperation in his voice. "I didn't choose the dress," she said. "Eldon's mother did."

"Who the hell is Eldon?"

"My fiancé."

"Oh, you mean the guy you left standing at the altar looking like a fool." He paused and glanced up at her. "Wouldn't it have been easier to just turn down his marriage proposal?"

"I did. A number of times. But my father wouldn't hear of it."

"Damn, these hooks are a pain in the butt," he muttered. "So you were marrying him because of your old man? Good reason."

Annie didn't miss the sarcasm in his voice. "It seemed like a good one at the time."

"Have you always done everything your daddy told you to do?"

"Pretty much. Are you almost finished?"

"Two more hooks to go."

"I meant are you almost finished interrogating me?"

He paused and found her gazing over her shoulder at him. "I don't have to do this, you know. I could leave you standing here on the side of the road."

Annie liked his hair. It was a rich dark brown. Any woman would ache to run her fingers through it. That, combined with his good looks, made her stomach flutter. "But you won't because you're a gentleman."

He grunted. "Boy, have you got me all wrong. Okay, I'm finished."

Holding the train over one arm, Annie did her best to fold it. She would have tossed it in the nearest trash can had she not promised to give it to Darla. "I think I'd do better if I sat in the backseat," she said.

He shrugged. "Suit yourself."

"You'll have to help me in."

"I never doubted it for a moment." Sam was glad the crowd had dispersed. Those few remaining were chatting among themselves, not paying any attention to the bride and her predicament. He opened the back door and stood aside for Annie to enter. Even without the train her dress was voluminous. She took a step up and tried to squeeze through the door. When it proved difficult, Sam placed his hands firmly on her rump and pushed. Annie went through the door, falling face first onto the backseat. Sam dusted his hands. "There now." He slammed the door, and a moment later climbed in on the driver's side.

Annie mouthed a couple of choice epithets as she tried to dig herself out of a mountain of satin and crinoline. "Why did you do that?" she sputtered.

Sam started the Jeep and pulled onto Main Street. "Because my patience has worn thin worrying about your dress problems. Now sit back and be quiet till we get to Darla's."

Annie was mad enough to spit, but she clamped her lips together tightly and ignored him as they made their way to the edge of town. Finally, Sam pulled off the main highway and drove down a dirt road, where an old mobile home sat beneath a stand of pines.

"This is where Darla lives?" she asked.

Sam pulled into a gravel drive and parked. "That's right. I know it doesn't look like much to a rich gal like you, but it's paid for and Darla loves it. Besides, you can't be too picky when she's giving you a place to stay for free."

Annie's feelings were hurt. "I don't know why you have to be so mean," she said. "I think Darla's place is just fine."

"Sure you do." He climbed out and opened the back door, then literally yanked her from the backseat.

Refusing to let him see how much he'd angered her, Annie made her way to the small porch attached to the trailer and unlocked the front door. The entrance was small, but worse than that, the metal on either side of the doorjamb was rusted and jagged. Going through the door would tear off at least half the tiny pearls that had been hand-sewn onto skirt.

"Now what?" Sam said, noting the problem. He was tempted to climb in his Jeep and leave Miss Fancy Pants right where she was. The only thing that kept him from doing that was the probability of Darla's wrath. Sometimes it was difficult trying to figure out which of them was the employer.

"Unzip me, please," Annie said, offering him her back.

He tilted his head to one side. "Excuse me?"

"I don't see any way to go through the doorway without damaging the dress, so the only alternative is to take it off. Unzip me," she repeated.

TWO

It wasn't easy getting her out of the dress; in fact, Sam suspected a straitjacket would have proved less difficult. But from the moment he ran the long zipper from the back of her neck almost to her tailbone, she had his undivided attention. Her skin was like alabaster dipped in rose petals, and her gently sloping shoulders cried out for a man's lips. The sight of her bra and panties stopped him cold. The wispy, flesh-colored fabric should have been outlawed. He drew in a sharp breath.

"What's wrong?" Annie said, stepping out of the dress. "Am I embarrassing you?" She might have been a little embarrassed herself had she not been hungry and irritable and downright determined to get out of the gown.

There was a faint tremor in his voice when he spoke. "Embarrassed is not exactly the word that comes to mind." She leaned forward to retrieve the dress, and Sam thought he would have a coronary when her lush breasts threatened to spill out of the lacy cups of her bra.

"You, uh, don't seem to have a problem with modesty," he noted.

"Would you rather I squeal and try to cover myself? Perhaps I could fake a case of the vapors." She shrugged. "Forget it. I'm not ashamed of my body, and I'm well acquainted with the male anatomy."

His gut tightened. "Oh."

"I grew up with an older brother and a whole slew of male cousins who thought nothing of shucking off their clothes for a cool swim in our lake. Before long, I was right alongside them. None of us ever thought anything about it."

"Then you fibbed to Sheriff Hester about being the only heir."

"My brother died more than ten years ago in a car accident."

"I'm sorry."

"Thank you." She noticed the way he was staring, and she couldn't help but find humor in the situation. "Is this the first time you've ever seen a woman in her underwear?"

He could feel the sweat beading on his brow, despite the cool September evening. "Yeah. And I may as well tell you, I'm disappointed as hell."

She nodded. "Sure you are." She turned and unlocked the door to the mobile home. She opened it, climbed the metal steps, and peered inside. "Oh, my."

Sam's eyes were still glued to her backside. "I forgot to tell you. Darla's a big Elvis fan."

"No kidding." Annie stepped inside, dragging the clump of satin with her. Elvis memorabilia cluttered the living room. A cheap plastic sofa table held at least two dozen decanters, each depicting the King at various stages in his life. There were personally autographed fan pictures hanging on the walls, snapshots and concert tickets tacked to a cork bulletin board. "Wow," she said. Sam stepped inside the room holding her slips, and it suddenly seemed to shrink in size.

"Darla belongs to some organization that is determined to prove Elvis is still alive," he said, trying not to stare at her scantily clad body. "They pay dues, and that money goes to a private investigator in Memphis who is scouting the country looking for him."

"We all need something to believe in," Annie said. She turned and found him staring. "Like what you see?"

His gaze climbed her body slowly, lazily, and he regarded her through half-closed lids. "I'm not going to apologize for admiring a beautiful woman."

Annie suddenly felt self-conscious. "I should get dressed," she said.

"Don't tell me you've suddenly had an attack of modesty."

"Of course not. But I don't like to be stared at like a side of beef."

"There's an easy solution for that, you know," he said, giving her a dazzling smile. "Put some clothes on."

Annie pressed her lips into a grim line and stalked through the kitchen and down the hall into what appeared to be the master bedroom. She tossed the wedding dress onto the bed, then remembering she'd made a gift of it to Darla, spread it out nicely and smoothed the wrinkles. She opened Darla's closet and felt she had just stepped into the sixties.

Sam tossed the slips on the sofa and sank into a chair.

For some reason or another, he sensed Miss High-and-Mighty in the next room didn't like him very much. And that didn't sit well with him, because most women, if not all, seemed to like him very much. Good looks aside, he was a successful attorney—well, as successful as one could be in a town the size of Pinckney—and an astute businessman to boot. 'Course, that wouldn't impress a woman like Annie Hartford, who probably came from old money and had never worked a day in her life.

Probably one of those highfalutin society queens whose only interest in a man was his breeding and the size of his bank account. A real Southern belle. He knew the type well. And what of Eldon, her betrothed? Probably a snob. Probably belonged to one of those private men's clubs that didn't permit women. Now, that was one thing Sam had never understood. What kind of man joined a club where there were no pretty women? Well, Eldon had certainly received a lesson in humility that day, what with his bride dumping him right in front of God and everybody. Actually, Sam felt a little sorry for him.

When she returned to the living room, Annie found Sam slumped in a chair, seemingly deep in thought. He took one look at the dress she wore and sat up. "It's a little short, isn't it?"

"I tried on several. They're all short. I see Darla likes big flowers. I feel like that girl from *The Mod Squad*."

"When did you ever watch *Mod Squad*? That was before your time."

"I watched the reruns when I was a kid."

"Yeah, you do kind of resemble Peggy Lipton in that outfit," he said with a chuckle. Only Annie was prettier.

Gorgeous, as far as he was concerned. But he wasn't about to tell her that. Just as he wouldn't tell her she had knockout legs and a tush that would bring most men to their knees. "Just don't bend over in that thing or you're liable to be attacked."

"Oh, really?" She looked amused. "Are you flirting with me, Mr. Ballard?"

He stood. He could have easily rested his chin on the top of her head. "No, ma'am," he said. "You'd be a handful for any man, and I don't like complications." He made for the door.

Annie frowned at the stinging remark. Outside, she locked up and pocketed the key in a large sunflower appliqué that was sewn to the dress. "Well, now. I do believe I've been rejected by Pinckney's most eligible bachelor. I hope you won't mind driving me to the nearest bridge so I can jump."

He laughed as he walked to his Jeep. "I must write Eldon and tell him what a lucky man he is."

Annie got in on the passenger's side. "Eldon is probably crying over a bottle of expensive scotch as we speak because he knows he's lost the best thing that ever happened to him."

Sam started the engine and backed out of the drive. "I can see you're all torn up about hurting your fiancé."

"Yes, Eldon will be quite bleary-eyed. You see, there are two things Eldon loves more than me. His scotch, and my daddy's money."

Sam glanced at her, and his look softened. "So that's the way it was, huh? And your father never saw through him?"

"My father thought the good Lord had sent Eldon to

replace the son he lost. There was no convincing him otherwise. But I don't want to talk about that anymore. I want to hear all about your life here in Pinckney. Do you have a girlfriend? I'll bet you have a dozen," she said, before he could answer. "I'll bet you've got one special girl, though, don't you? Let me guess. Her name is Lulu, and she waits tables at the local bowling alley. She's got boobs the size of cantaloupes, and a pea-sized brain. Am I right?"

Sam turned onto the main road leading into town. "You know, just as I think I could like you, you go and blow it for me."

"I sure hope we make it to that bridge soon," she quipped.

They made the rest of the drive in silence. When Sam parked in front of the Dixieland Café, Annie politely thanked him and climbed out. "Give Lulu my best," she said before closing the door.

Sam shook his head as he watched Annie walk into his restaurant. The woman was an enigma. And what a mouth. If she were his, he'd take great pleasure in turning her over his knee. But the mere thought of spanking that pert behind gave him an erection.

Darla whistled when she spied Annie in her dress. "Kinda short on you, ain't it? Too bad you're not waiting tables, we'd have to get a Brink's truck to haul your tips home. You want a cup of coffee?"

"I'd love it." Once Darla had set a steaming cup before her, Annie waved her away. "Go wait on your other customers, I'll be okay."

"You like fried chicken?" Darla asked. When Annie nodded, she scribbled out the order on her pad. "Saturday is fried-chicken night, and our cook, Miss Flo, makes the best in the word. Her daughter, Patricia, makes the biscuits from scratch."

"Sounds good," Annie replied. Actually, she would have eaten soggy cardboard at the moment, since she hadn't put a thing in her stomach all day. She'd been too nervous before the wedding, then far too upset after fleeing the scene. She had done a very stupid thing waiting until she was about to walk down the aisle before backing out. But even if she had protested marrying Eldon it wouldn't have done any good; her father had been determined. Guilt was a powerful weapon if used correctly, and her father had been guilt-tripping her all her life for one reason or another.

Annie had to agree with Darla's assessment of the chicken when she tasted it some minutes later. It was crisp on the outside and so tender inside, it almost melted in her mouth. It was served with mashed potatoes and gravy, seasoned green beans, and a mouthwatering biscuit. "Wow," was all she said, when Darla picked up her plate. "Tell Flo and Patricia I want to be adopted into their family."

"You'll think twice about that when you find out what kind of temper Flo has," Darla warned her. "She threw a skillet at me once, and if I hadn't ducked, she would have taken my head clean off. Got after Sam with a knife when he refused to give her a raise. She left that night making fifty cents an hour more."

"Whatever it takes to keep up with the cost of living," Annie said with a chuckle.

"You probably wouldn't know much about that," Darla replied. "You look like you come from money."

"Money can't buy happiness," Annie said.

Darla gave a snort. "Spoken like a true rich person."

Annie glanced around as the front door opened and half a dozen women walked in. "We want our regular table," one of them said.

Darla saluted. "I'm acomin' with fresh hot coffee."

"Who are those ladies?" Annie asked.

"The Pinckney Social Club. They come in every Saturday night for Flo's chicken. Most are widowed or divorced. Come on over, I want you to meet them." When Annie protested, Darla became insistent. "You'll like them."

Annie followed reluctantly. "Hey, everybody," Darla said. "I want y'all to meet Annie Hartford. She arrived in town late this afternoon driving a limo and wearing a wedding gown."

"Oh, honey, we heard all about it," a petite, middle-aged woman with frosted hair said. "Sit down and tell us everything." She pulled out the chair next to her, and Annie sat. "By the way, my name is Lillian Calhoun," she said, offering her hand. Annie shook it, noting as she did, several fingers blazed with diamonds.

"Everybody calls her Diamond Lil," Darla said. "I don't reckon you need an explanation."

"It just so happens Sam Ballard got me a dandy divorce settlement," Lillian said. "Everybody kept telling me to get one of those highfalutin attorneys in Athens, but I wouldn't have thought of using anyone but Sam. Besides, where else can you get your legal work taken care of and look for a used car too?"

"When's the last time you bought a used car, Lillian Calhoun?" Darla said, and the group erupted into laughter. She turned to Annie. "You're looking at a woman who buys a custom Mercedes every two years."

"Have to keep my expenses high if I expect to keeping getting those fat alimony checks," Lillian replied.

"Well, your rings are beautiful," Annie said. She knew good-quality stones when she saw them, and Lillian's were top of the line.

The woman leaned close. "Truth to tell, there aren't enough diamonds in the world to repay me for the heartache I've known. I gave that man the best years of my life, worked my tail off so I could help him get through med school. Gave him three fine sons. And how does he repay me? By running off with his scrub nurse."

"So you were married to a doctor?"

"A surgeon. Has a practice in Athens. I came to live in Pinckney after the divorce because I have a sister here. She's married to a wonderful man. He doesn't have much money, but he treats her like a queen, and that's what counts." She suddenly looked embarrassed. "But I'm monopolizing the conversation. You have to meet the rest of the girls.

"That pretty Asian woman sitting next to you is Kazue Hitchcock."

A dark-headed woman introduced herself as Cheryl Camp who worked in human resources, and the woman sitting across from her, by the name of Inge Mercer, welcomed Annie to town.

"Inge isn't allowed to smoke in the house," Cheryl said, "so she's joined every organization this town has to offer so she can get out and puff her stuff."

"It's not that I can't smoke," Inge objected. "I just don't do it because my husband has allergies."

"Did you really sneak out of the church and steal your father's limo to get away?" Kazue asked Annie. "That's what everybody is talking about."

Annie nodded, but she was embarrassed that everyone in town already knew about her escape. "I suppose it was rather cowardly of me."

"Bull!" Inge shook her head emphatically. "You did the right thing, honey. You can't marry a man just because your daddy says so. There comes a time when you have to stand up for your rights."

"I'd say Annie did a very good job of standing up for herself today," Cheryl said. She handed Annie her business card. "You may need some counseling after this. You call me, and I'll set you up with someone."

Just then, Darla, who'd disappeared to check on her other customers, returned. "Everybody want the fried-chicken special tonight?" she asked.

"That's why we're here," Lillian replied.

"Oh, I thought y'all came to see me," a male voice chimed in. Annie glanced around to find Sam Ballard standing behind her.

"Oh, there's my handsome lawyer," Lillian said. Sam walked over and kissed her on the cheek.

"I believe you have a new bauble, Mrs. Calhoun," he said, checking her pinkie finger.

Lil waved the statement aside. "Oh, that's just a little something I picked up on a recent Hilton Head visit."

"What are you going to do when you run out of fingers?"

"I'm going to put a ring in my navel," she said, and the group laughed.

Sam glanced at Annie and his smile faded, but his gaze

lingered. "Well, I'll leave you ladies to your dinner. I'm sure you have a lot of catching up to do since last week."

Nobody spoke until he walked away. Finally, Lillian nudged Annie. "What was *that* all about?"

"You mean the dirty look?" She shrugged. "I don't think Mr. Ballard cares for me very much. You know, running out on my wedding the way I did."

"Oh, yes," Inge said. "The same thing happened to him."

Lillian shook her head. "Not exactly. His fiancée broke it off several days before the wedding."

"That's no reason for him to dislike you," Cheryl said. "I'm sure the circumstances were completely different. Besides, it's none of his business."

Darla showed up with their salads. "Y'all haven't managed to corrupt Annie yet, have you?"

Lillian laughed. "Corrupt her? Darla, we wouldn't think of it. Why, she's like a fresh new magnolia blossom. How old are you, Annie? Twenty-five?"

"I'll be thirty my next birthday."

"Say it ain't so," Cheryl cried.

Darla set the last salad down. "She's rich. Rich people age slower than the rest of us."

Annie shook her head. "My father's rich. But he's probably written me out of his will by now. So now I'm poor, homeless, and unemployed."

"Spoken like a true rich person," Inge said as she attacked her salad.

Darla returned with the coffeepot and freshened their coffee. "I've made a mess of everything," Annie said, feeling suddenly hopeless. "I never should have done what I did today. I should have broken off the engagement long ago."

"It's in the past now," Cheryl told her. "You can feel guilty if you like, but that won't get you anywhere. You need to go forward now."

"And no looking back," Lillian said. "So you don't have a place to stay?"

"I can stay with Darla for the time being."

"Hope you like Elvis," Inge muttered.

"Okay, so you have a place to stay at least temporarily," Cheryl said. "Now you'll need to find some kind of job. Problem is, this is a small town and jobs are hard to come by. But I have a good friend who runs a job service, so who knows? What kind of work do you do?"

Annie thought about it. "I've never really worked. I never even went to a real college, if you want to know the truth. Just that dumb ol' finishing school."

"Well, you've had to be doing something since then," Inge said.

Annie shrugged. "I took care of my father's house, and I planned dinner parties for him."

The women at the table stared at her, mouths agape. "Okay, don't panic," Lillian said. "I'm sure there's something she can do." She patted Annie's hand. "Each of us was blessed with a special talent. Look at me, I never worked a day in my life while I was married. All I did was shop and have lunch with my friends. Of course, I kept our home looking like a showplace, and there was always a magnificent dinner on the table when His Highness walked through the door.

"The one thing I enjoyed was decorating. And I was good at it. Friends were always coming to me for ideas and suggestions. So when I moved to Pinckney, I opened a small decorating business. And Kazue, who had an alterations shop next door, began making window treatments and bedspreads for my clients. Shoot, we're as busy as a one-armed paper hanger now."

"Honey, you may have to start at the bottom and work your way up," Inge said.

"What would the bottom be?" Annie asked curiously, hoping it wouldn't entail taking her clothes off.

"You can make beds, can't you?"

"I'm sure I could if somebody showed me how."

Inge dropped her fork. "You've never made a bed?"

"Yes, I did," Annie suddenly said with some excitement. "At summer camp one year. We all had to make our own beds." She looked proud. The others were speechless.

"What's wrong here?" Darla asked, arriving with their fried-chicken dinners.

"Oh, we were just discussing what kind of job Annie might be able to find in Pinckney. She doesn't have much experience."

"I've already thought about the job situation," Darla told them. "I'm going to get Sam to hire her on here."

Annie looked surprised. "You mean as a waitress?" When Darla nodded, she went on. "I've never done that before."

"Then you're very lucky that you're going to be trained by the best," Darla informed her.

Annie glanced around. Sam was having coffee with a customer. They seemed to be deep in conversation. As though sensing he was being watched, his gaze slid in her direction. His eyes narrowed in suspicion as to why she was watching him. He was the first to look away.

"He doesn't even like me," she said.

"You've got to stop thinking negative thoughts like that, Annie," Darla told her. "Besides, Sam does everything I tell him to do. He doesn't always know it. Sometimes I let him think it's his idea, but I'm the one who planted it there to begin with. I may not be doing you a big favor getting you a job at the Dixieland Café. The work is hard, but as I see it, you're desperate." She paused. "Unless you want to return home."

"No, I can't do that," Annie said quickly. "I don't know if I can ever go back."

"Then you just leave the rest to me," Darla said.

THREE

"No. Absolutely not. You must be out of your mind to even suggest such a thing."

Darla studied Sam as he counted the day's earnings from the cash register and made out a deposit slip. They were alone; the cook had left moments before. Lillian had driven Annie back to Darla's place, and the waitress felt it was as good a time as any to ask Sam to hire the girl. "Sam, just tell me this. What do you have against Annie?"

"I don't even know the woman, how can I have anything against her?"

"Then what have you got against me?"

He looked up in surprise. "Now, that's a dumb question if ever there was one. I don't have the first thing against you. Why would you even ask such a thing?"

"You obviously don't care about my health. And if you don't care about my health, then—"

Now he looked frustrated. "What in Sam Hill are you talking about? What's wrong with your health?"

"I'm getting old."

"You're thirty-five, for Pete's sake. That's not old. Anybody who can dance all night at that redneck bar on the edge of town, then come in the next day and work a double shift is definitely not old. You're in your prime, Darla Mae Jenkins."

"I can't keep up like I used to. I have corns on my feet trying to run this place by myself. Hell, my corns have corns. Do you know how unattractive that is, Sam? Why do you think I had to go buy that expensive new garter belt? It's to keep men looking there and not at my feet."

"Maybe you should slow down on your, uh, extracurricular activities. Why don't you try going to bed with a good book once in a while instead of dragging home something in tight jeans and cowboy boots?"

"Do you go to bed every night with a good book, Sam?" she asked.

"Most nights I do." When she gave a snort, he looked at her. "I'm thirty-five years old, too, honey. My hell-raising days are over. Besides, I'm not into taking risks."

"My love life is not what matters at the moment. When I leave this restaurant my time is my own. The fact is, you promised to hire someone before the Okra Festival, and now it's less than a week away. You know what that's like. There is absolutely no way I can handle those crowds by myself."

He sighed. "Tell you what I'll do. I'll run an ad in the newspaper."

"Forget it. By the time someone responds, I can have Annie trained. The festival starts a week from yesterday."

"Then I'll find someone with experience."

Darla's lips were pressed into a grim line as she reached beneath the counter for her purse. "Good night, Sam."

He glanced up, surprised. "What, you're not even going to wait for me?"

"I've waited long enough." She unlocked the front door and walked out without another word.

Annie was waiting for Darla when she arrived home. "What'd he say?"

Darla dropped her bag on the floor and slumped into a chair. "He's going to think about it."

"Well, that's better than saying no."

"I'm beat," Darla muttered.

"Can I get you something from the kitchen? A hot chocolate, maybe?"

Darla gave her a weary smile. "No, I'm fine. In a few minutes I'll be good as new. Take me a hot shower, probably want to drive over to Ernie's."

"Who's Ernie?"

Darla chuckled. "It's not a who, it's a place. Just a little waterin' hole on the edge of town. I usually go have a cold beer and it relaxes me so I can come back and get some sleep. Hey, you might be interested in going. Meet some of my friends. It's only nine-thirty, and it's Saturday night. The place'll be hoppin'."

Annie couldn't help but wonder what kind of place Ernie's was, but the last thing she wanted to do was hurt Darla's feelings. "Sure, I'll go. Do I need to change clothes?"

"Most folks wear jeans. It's a country-western bar."

"Your jeans are too short on me."

"I've got a pair that need hemming. They'll probably do."

The two women were on their way in a matter of minutes. Although Annie was exhausted and would have preferred climbing into a comfortable bed, she figured it would be rude not to go with the woman who was offering her a place to stay. Besides, it was to her advantage to meet as many people as she could, since the subject of her employment wasn't yet settled. She was more than a little nervous at the thought of working at the Dixieland Café. What did she know about waitress work? But then, what did she know about anything?

It was her own fault for not standing up to her father years ago when she was planning her education. She should never have let him send her to some dumb finishing school, where the staff was more interested in teaching her to set a lovely table or plan a party for one hundred guests than how to support herself.

Her own fault. Now here she was, almost thirty years old, and didn't have a clue what she was going to do with her life. The only thing she knew for certain was that she had no intention of marrying Eldon-the-Chosen-One, or even returning home anytime soon. She might not have gone about it the right way, but then she'd never had the opportunity to make her own decisions. Nevertheless, what was done was done, and her father and Eldon could sit and stew in their own juices for all she cared.

Annie frowned when Darla pulled into the parking lot of a large one-story cinderblock building. The place was surrounded by motorcycles and pickup trucks, some of the trucks so high off the ground, it would have taken a stepladder for her to reach the door. "Is this it?" she asked, although a massive neon sign flashing beside the road clearly spelled out ERNIE'S PLACE.

"This is it," Darla said, parking beside a truck with a Confederate flag draped across the back window. "Do I look okay?"

Annie wasn't sure how to respond to someone wearing a leather miniskirt, tank-top blouse, and a blue-jean jacket. "Let's just put it this way, Darla. You will definitely stand out in a crowd in that outfit."

The woman smiled. "Thanks, darlin'. That's just the kind of thing a girl likes to hear. Come on. Let's play."

Annie climbed out of the car and followed Darla toward the building with mounting trepidation. If the music blaring outside the building was any indication of how loud it was inside, she knew she was in for a long night. But her poor eardrums were not prepared for the moment when Darla opened the door, or the loud squeal Darla gave the moment they stepped inside.

At first Annie thought her friend had hurt herself somehow, but a second later Darla threw her arms around a man's neck. Annie decided the woman must be very happy to see him. And he to see her, from the way he picked her up and swung her around as if she were a sack of flour. The two carried on for a good five minutes while Annie stood there wondering what to do with herself.

"Hank, it's so good to see you," Darla said, giving him another hug. She glanced at Annie as though realizing for the first time she was standing there. "Oh, I want you to meet my new roommate, honey. This here's

Annie. Annie, meet Hank, my old boyfriend. We go way back."

Annie smiled and offered her hand, but Hank obviously decided a bear hug was more appropriate. By the time he set her down, Annie was certain all the bones in her body had been crushed.

"C'mon and let me buy you pretty gals a cold one," he said, dragging them toward a bar that ran the entire length of the room. Darla had to pause a number of times to speak to someone and introduce Hank and Annie. By the time they reached the bar, Annie's head was splitting from the music.

"What'll it be, miss?" the bartender asked her. He wore overalls and looked as though he'd been plowing a field all day.

"Just give me a diet soft drink," she said, and received a good deal of ribbing from Darla and Hank, both of whom ordered a draft beer. Annie had barely managed to take a sip before a tall red-haired man named Jesse tapped her on the shoulder and asked her to dance. She turned him down, only to have Darla insist she dance with him because he was a friend of hers. Annie soon found herself trying to keep time to a tune with fiddle music and before long she had more dance partners than she knew what to do with.

Sam was surprised to find Darla's lights off and the car gone when he pulled into the driveway of her mobile home. She'd rushed out of the restaurant in such a hurry that she'd forgotten her wallet. She pulled it out when she'd cashed her tips out at the end of the night, exchanging change and small bills so he wouldn't have to worry about going to the bank to replenish it. He knew she was ticked off at him, and he knew why, but he couldn't go hiring someone to work at the restaurant just because Darla said so.

It didn't take Sam long to figure out where the two women had gone. With it being Saturday night, he knew his star waitress would be sitting in Ernie's. 'Course tomorrow she'd be as hungover as a Shriner at an annual convention, and the church crowd would have her hopping like a barefoot young'un on a hot sidewalk. She'd be in a sour mood and probably get into it with Flo.

Sam had no desire to go to Ernie's, but he knew he had to get Darla's wallet to her, despite her frequent bragging about never paying for a drink. Sam backed out of the drive, and as he headed in the direction of the redneck hangout, he tried to imagine Annie in such a place. He couldn't.

Pleading exhaustion to her current dance partner, Annie returned to the bar, only to find Darla and Hank missing. The bartender in overalls returned wearing a grin. "Some of your dance partners have taken a shine to you," he said. "They want to buy you a drink. Several, in fact. What'll you have?"

"I don't want anything right now," Annie replied as politely as she could, considering her head felt as though it was ready to split open. "Would you happen to know where my friend went?"

"She left with that other feller. Said to tell you'd she'd be back in a jiffy."

"When you see her, would you please tell her I'm waiting for her in the car?"

"What do I look like, Western Union?"

"I'm sorry to impose—"

"I'm just havin' fun with you," he said, his chubby face breaking into a grin. "I'll tell her."

Annie made her way out the door, leaving a good portion of the noise inside. She passed a couple of men sitting on the tailgate of a truck but pretended not to see them.

"Hey, baby, you lookin' for some comp'ny?"

"No thanks," she said, and kept on walking.

"Hey, that ain't no way to be," one of them said as he caught up with her. "What'd I ever do to you?"

"Please—" She stopped and turned. He was a beefy fellow, but he wasn't dressed in biker's clothes, and Annie felt that was in her favor. He spit a wad of chewing tobacco on the ground, and she shuddered. "I have a splitting headache, and I just want to be alone," she said. She resumed walking. Where the hell had Darla parked?

"I got a headache powder in the truck."

Sure he did, Annie thought. And she had a hundred-dollar bill in her pocket.

It finally hit her that Darla's car was missing, and the thought of being stranded at a place like Ernie's almost made her weep. Why would Darla have left her? Especially knowing she didn't have a dime to her name? She didn't even have enough money to call anyone. Besides, who would she call?

"You can drink it down with a cold beer, and that headache'll be history."

Annie saw a car turn off the highway into the parking

lot, and she prayed it was Darla's. She almost went weak with relief when it turned out to be a Jeep driven by Sam Ballard. He pulled up beside her.

"Out slumming tonight, Annie?"

"I beg your pardon?"

"If you're looking for trouble, this is the place to find it." Sam slammed the Jeep into park and climbed out. Annie noticed the stranger's friend had come up; both of them towered over Sam.

"I asked you what the hell you're doing and who these men are?" he almost shouted.

Annie's jaw dropped. "I don't have to take this—"

The man next to Annie nudged her. "Do you know this guy?"

"Yes, I—"

"I happen to be her husband," Sam said, his words clipped and precise. "She has a new baby at home waiting to be nursed. She told me she was running to the store for disposable diapers."

"Oh, well—" The man looked from Sam to Annie and back to Sam. "Hey, man, we don't want to cause no trouble between married folks. Me and my brother was just passing through town." He regarded Annie. "You should be home with your kid, lady." He looked at the other man. "C'mon, let's get outta here."

Annie was glad it was dark and nobody could see the crimson color on her face. "That was despicable," she told Sam.

"Would you rather see me get beat up by the rhino brothers?" He didn't give her time to answer. "Where's Darla, and what the hell are you doing in a dark parking lot with some men you don't know?"

"I don't know where Darla is, and I don't have to answer your questions."

"Great. Then I'll just leave you here to fend for yourself." He turned and climbed back inside the Jeep.

"Wait!" Annie hurried over. "Darla's car is gone. She took off with some guy named Hank."

"So you decided to wait for her in a parking lot filled with drunk rednecks and bikers. Great idea, Annie. Now I see why your father had to make your decisions for you all your life." He regretted his choice of words the minute they left his mouth, the very second he saw Annie's face fall. But, dammit, she could have gotten in bad trouble there.

Sudden tears stung her eyes. "You can just go straight to hell for all I care." She started walking.

He pulled up beside her. "I'm sorry, Annie. That was a lousy thing for me to say. Get in the car, and I'll take you back to Darla's."

"Just leave me alone. I'd rather walk."

"You can't walk. It's dangerous this time of night."

"I can take care of myself. Contrary to what you might think."

They had reached the highway. "I'll bet you don't even know how to get to Darla's trailer."

Annie wasn't listening. It had been such a miserable day, not to mention humiliating as hell, and her head felt as though it would explode. She had spent the better part of the evening wondering what she was going to do with her life and cursing the fact that she hadn't taken charge long ago. The last thing she needed was for Sam Ballard to show up and rub her nose in it.

"Annie, I'm warning you, either get in, or I'll personally put you in."

She kept walking.

Sam gunned his engine and parked a good distance ahead of her. He climbed out, then slammed the door so hard, his Jeep rocked on its wheels. Teeth gritted, he closed the distance between him and Annie, then, without warning, hefted her up and threw her over his shoulder. She kicked and squealed like a stuck pig.

"Shut up, dammit!" he ordered. "Folks'll think I'm kidnapping you." She screamed louder, and he gave her a sound whack on the behind.

Annie saw red. She kicked her legs and flailed her arms and finally grabbed a handful of his hair. Sam let a few obscenities fly before he realized someone had pulled up behind them. He turned but was blinded by headlights. He blinked several times before he realized it was the highway patrol.

"Dammit to hell, Annie, look what you've done now." He heard the door open and close, was barely able to make out the silhouette of a patrolman.

"What's going on here?" the uniformed man said.

Annie continued to pummel Sam in the back but glanced around at the sound of another's voice. "Oh, Officer, thank God you're here. I'm being abducted."

"Abducted, huh?" The patrolman spit what looked like a wad of chewing tobacco on the ground, and Annie wondered if everybody in Pinckney chewed it. "Well, we don't put up with the likes of that in Pinckney, ma'am." He reached for his gun. "I reckon I don't have any choice but to shoot him."

FOUR

In disbelief, Annie watched the patrolman pull his gun out of the holster and aim it at Sam. She screamed. "No, wait!"

"Put her down, pal," the armed man said. "I'm warning you, I got this sucker aimed right for your goozle."

Sam sighed heavily and dropped Annie to the ground. She landed in a heap.

"Now move away, lady, so I can finish him off."

"Officer, please let me explain," Annie cried, crawling along the gravel as fast as she could. She pulled herself up by the man's pants leg. "He, uh, Mr. Ballard here, was only offering me a ride. I was lying about being abducted."

"He probably told you to say that, didn't he?" The patrolman pushed her aside. "You need to turn your head, miss. I've done this sort of thing before, and it ain't a pretty sight."

"Oh, my God, no!" Annie threw herself in front of Sam, acting as a shield.

Sam stood there with his arms crossed over his chest, the lines in his face tense, as if holding himself in check while Annie sobbed and carried on like a character in a bad soap opera. "Okay, Buster, you've had your fun. I'd like to go home now."

The other man chuckled and stuck his revolver back in its holster. "Listen, Sambo, you're going to have to learn to start charming the ladies a little better. You can't just throw a woman over your shoulder like a sack of taters and haul her off. You have to buy them flowers and candy and—" He paused and looked around as though wanting to make sure they weren't overheard. "You might have to write a few lines of poetry. It don't matter if it don't rhyme."

Annie's head swiveled from side to side. "Excuse me, but do you two know each other?"

Sam looked at her. "This is Johnny Ballard, my cousin. Folks call him Buster. He's a real prankster."

"So all this was just a big joke at my expense," she said. She glared at Sam. "You let me grovel and beg for your life like some idiot nutcase. How dare you!"

A car screeched to a halt, and Darla jumped out and came running. She looked panicked. "What's wrong? Is somebody hurt?"

"Well, now, ain't you a sight for sore eyes," Buster said. "Why don't you and me go for a spin in my patrol car. I'll even let you play with my siren."

"Annie, what's going on?" Darla asked.

Annie tried to explain everything that had happened since she'd last seen her friend. It was all she could do to get the words out, what with her stammering and sputtering. Her heart was still racing.

"Didn't the bartender give you my message?" Darla asked. "Hank needed cigarettes, and we drove up to the convenience store. I told the bartender to tell you I'd be right back. Only, I didn't know Hank was going to hang around and look at dirty magazines."

"Would you please take me home?" Annie asked, realizing that she was trembling. "You're welcome to go back to Ernie's and stay as long as you like, but I'm exhausted."

"Sure, honey. We can go."

"I'll walk back," Hank said, having come up in the meantime. He kissed Darla on the cheek. "I'll call you, babe."

Buster put his hand on Annie's shoulder. "I hope I didn't scare you, young lady. Sam and I are always cutting up."

"Actually, I think the whole scene was disgraceful," she said. "I hope you have your little notebook handy because I want to file assault-and-battery charges."

Buster looked startled as he reached into his pocket. "Is this for real?"

Making a fist with one hand, Annie swung around and slammed it into Sam Ballard's face. She heard a sickening *thwack*, felt the pain explode in her knuckles, and wondered if she'd merely managed to break the bones in her own hand. Sam, who had not been expecting to be punched, fell flat on his back on the ground.

Buster hurried over to the fallen man. "Hey, Sambo, are you okay?"

Sam raised up and shook his head to clear it. "Damn, she knocked me on my butt." He glared at Annie, who looked quite pleased with herself.

"She sure did," Buster said. "That's assault and battery if I ever saw it. You want to press charges? 'Course, you know folks're going to tease you something fierce about being beat up by a girl."

"Buster—" Sam tried to interrupt.

"The good news is they'll probably forget about that nasty business when your bride-to-be skipped town only hours before y'all were supposed to walk down the aisle. Hey, buddy, I'm with you no matter what you decide."

"Just get her out of my sight," Sam told Buster.

"Don't bother," Annie said. "I'm out of here." She spun around on her heels and stalked toward Darla's car.

Annie was still fuming the next morning as she replayed in her mind the good-ol'-boy routine she'd witnessed the night before between Sam and his cousin. And to think, she had tried to shield Sam's body with her own to keep Buster from shooting him! They were probably still laughing over the whole thing. She had done nothing but make a gigantic fool of herself since she'd rolled into town in a smoking limo, wearing enough satin to make sheets for everyone in Pinckney.

She would never be able to hold her head up in front of the townspeople. They'd probably insist she wear the words TOWN IDIOT embroidered on her blouse.

Annie heard the floor creak and turned as Darla staggered down the hall looking like something the cat would refuse to drag in. "What's wrong?" she asked.

"I'm sick," Darla said. "I think it's the flu."

"Oh no. Can I get you something?"

"You can go get my shotgun out of the closet in my bedroom and put me out of my misery."

"Sit down, and I'll pour you a cup of coffee," Annie said, getting up from her chair. Darla made it to the sofa and collapsed. "Do you have any cold medicine on hand?"

"No. I never get sick." She coughed and moaned. "I haven't been sick since—" She paused. "I don't remember when."

Annie poured the coffee and carried it to her friend. "You take it black, right?"

Darla mumbled something to the affirmative. "What time is it?" she asked as she raised the cup to her lips.

"Ten o'clock."

"I'm supposed to be at work by ten forty-five to set up for the lunch crowd. There's no way I can make it feeling like this. You'll have to go in for me, Annie."

"Me!" Annie almost shrieked the word. "But I don't know the first thing about waitress work."

"You said yourself how you used to plan big parties for your father's friends and clients," Darla pointed out. "All you have to do is smile at everybody and try to get along with Flo and Patricia. If you make them mad, you're screwed."

"Shouldn't I call Sam first and tell him you're sick? Let him make the decision?"

"He probably won't even be there. There's an older woman who works the breakfast crowd. Sam only comes in to fill his thermos with coffee, then he goes back to his office across the street." Darla paused. "You have to do this for me, Annie. I could lose my job, and somebody *has* to be there to serve those customers."

Annie was truly torn. After losing her temper and punching Sam in the face, he might just wring her neck when he saw her again. "What am I supposed to wear?"

"I have a couple of clean uniforms in my closet."

Annie checked her wristwatch. There wasn't much time to argue, considering she had to take a shower and put on a little makeup. She took a deep breath. "Okay, I'll do it. He may toss me out of the place the minute he sees me, but I'll give it my best shot." She was already headed in the direction of the bathroom.

Annie showered and dressed in record time, then applied her makeup quickly and sparingly. The uniform was too short—no surprise there—but there wasn't much she could do about it at the moment. She started for the front door, promising to call and check on Darla later, then it hit her. "Oh, no. How am I supposed to get to work?"

"My car keys are on the kitchen table."

"But I don't have my license and Sheriff Hester—"

"Forget about him. Just park the car in the back of the restaurant. You can tell him I drove you. He's not likely to take you in and interrogate you."

Shaking her head and wondering how her life had become so confused, Annie grabbed the keys and hurried out to Darla's car. It was in sad shape. The seats had been taped and stitched so many times, it resembled a patchwork quilt. Annie thought of the Mercedes SL her father had given her after graduating from Twyla Pettibone's Finishing School, and the white Jaguar presently sitting in the driveway at home, and she realized she had always taken those things for granted.

Never again. She saw how hard Darla had to work just

to cover the bare essentials. Annie wanted more out of life. She didn't have to be rich, and she didn't have to drive a fancy foreign car, but she wanted the security of knowing she could make it on her own. Just like Lillian Calhoun and Kazue and the others, who'd proved to everyone, as well as to themselves, that they had what it took to survive in this world.

Annie was still deep in thought when she pulled into the driveway in back of the Dixieland Café. She was a few minutes early, but it would give her time to get everything set up just right. She pushed through the back door and found herself in the kitchen with Flo and Patricia, neither of whom looked particularly pleased to see her. Her former resolve started to slip.

"Who the hell are you?" Flo asked, pausing in her work to scrutinize her.

"My name's Annie, and I desperately need your help."

Patricia put a fist on her hip and cocked her head to the side. "Oh, yeah?"

"Darla's sick, and there's nobody to take over but me. But I don't know the first thing about waiting tables. I was hoping the two of you could show me the ropes, so to speak."

The two women exchanged looks. Flo cocked her head to the side. "Does Sam know about this?"

"No. He would probably toss me out of this kitchen if he saw me here."

"He ain't gonna toss you out of *my* kitchen," Flo said. "If he so much as tries, the last thing he'll see in my behind going out the back door."

"Then you'll help me?" Annie asked, a pleading note in her voice.

Flo sighed heavily. Patricia pressed her lips together in a grim line. "I'll help you as much as I can," Flo said, "but I got my own job to do, too, you know. Right now you need to go out and talk to Gladys, the breakfast waitress. She can show you what you'll need to do."

Annie thanked them profusely, pushed through the swinging doors, and came face-to-face with a squatty, thick-waisted woman with gray hair and thick-framed glasses. Her pale yellow uniform was as crisp as a brand-new linen tablecloth, but her shoes made annoying squashing and sucking noises when she walked.

"Who are you?" she asked.

"Annie Hartford. I'm covering for Darla today. She's got the flu."

"Most likely it's a hangover."

"No, I saw her myself. She's really sick."

Gladys sighed as though the world had just settled on her shoulders. "Okay, let me show you around. I reckon I can help you set up for lunch. I might as well warn you, it gets a little busy once the church crowd hits. But we won't have to worry about that after today because Sam has decided to start closing on Sunday, thanks to me and Darla ragging him all the time. Folks need at least one day a week off."

Annie agreed wholeheartedly with the crusty waitress and thought she'd scored a few points with her. By the time the church crowd arrived, she had received a crash course in waitressing from Gladys and the girls in the kitchen and was breathless and jittery. But she kept telling herself to smile, write her order legibly, and smile some more. She politely ignored the table of teenage boys who kept dropping their forks so she would have to stoop down in her short skirt to retrieve them. She felt she was doing an okay job until Sam Ballard walked through the door. One sight of him and the shiner on his right eye and Annie lost control of the small tray she was carrying. Four iced-tea glasses crashed to the floor, causing everyone in the restaurant to jump and search for the source of the commotion. Annie immediately went down on all fours to collect the broken glass.

"Don't touch that!" Sam said, his voice ringing loud with command. "You'll cut yourself."

Too late. Annie winced as a shard of glass jabbed her right index finger.

Sam knelt beside her, his look thunderous. "What the hell are you doing here?" he demanded.

A wave of apprehension coursed through her. Why had Darla just assumed she could saunter into the place ready for work without talking to Sam first? "Darla's sick. She asked me to cover for her."

His eyes darkened as he held her gaze. "Oh, she did, did she?" he asked, mockery invading his tone. "Well, she can look for another job after today."

"But—"

He wasn't listening. "Go in the kitchen and ask Flo to take care of your finger. I'll clean this up. Then I want you out of here."

"Who's going to wait on these tables?"

Annoyance hovered in his eyes. "That's not your problem now, is it?"

She tried to disguise her own annoyance in front of the customers. "You're mean and hateful, Sam Ballard, you know that? Is it a sin for one of your employees to get sick?"

He stiffened, as though she'd just punched him in the eye again. His look seemed to drill right through her. "Darla's not sick. This is all just a ruse for her to get her way. Besides, it's none of your business how I treat my employees."

She was unnerved by his hostility, and wished now that she'd slugged him in both eyes. The man was truly insufferable. Deciding it would be best to hold her tongue and walk away from the situation, Annie stood and hurried toward the kitchen.

Flo took one look at her and grabbed a first-aid kit. "That glass went pretty deep," she said, once she'd cleaned the wound. "Wouldn't hurt to have a stitch or two in it."

"I don't have time to go to the hospital," Annie said. "Just do the best you can." Her voice cracked.

Patricia came over. "What's wrong with you? You gonna cry over a little cut like that?"

"That's not it," Annie said, then blurted the whole story. "Sam told me to get out, and he said he was going to fire Darla."

"Fire her?" Flo said angrily. "Over my dead body." She finished wrapping the finger and checked her work.

"Why do you care?" Patricia asked. "You don't even like the woman."

"I ain't got nary a thing against Darla Jenkins 'cept for that smart-aleck mouth of hers. But Sam ain't got no right to fire an employee just because she's sick. What's going to happen if one of us gets sick? We gonna get canned too?"

Sam came into the kitchen with the tray of broken glass just as Flo and Patricia clocked out and started for the back door. "Where do you two think you're going?" he said, dumping the glass into a trash can.

"We quit," Patricia said.

"Wait just a damn minute!" he ordered, stopping both women in their tracks. "What's this all about?"

They did a double take at the sight of his bruised eye. "We just heard you plan to fire Darla for being sick. And that you're sending this poor child home after she came in and did her level best to take over when there was no one else."

Sam shot an accusing look at Annie. "You just got to cause trouble for me wherever you go, don't you?" he said.

She crossed her arms and pointedly stared. "If you think I'm going to keep quiet when you threaten my friend's job, you're wrong," she said matter-of-factly. "And if you think I'm going to put up with some ill-mannered oaf, you're wrong there too. I was only trying to help out because there was no one to work in Darla's place."

"And she was doing a fine job of it till you came in and stirred things up," Patricia said.

"I suppose I'm to overlook what you did to my eye," Sam told Annie.

Flo's own eyes widened. "You popped him in the eye?"

Annie nodded. "He played a very cruel joke on me."

"Then he obviously had it coming. I ought to take my frying pan to you, Sam Ballard," Flo said. "What's gotten into you?"

Just then a tall bearded fellow pushed open the swinging door. "What do you have to do to get served in this place?" he demanded.

Sam pasted a smile on his face. "Sorry, sir, we had a little emergency. I'll be right out." He appealed to Flo and Patricia. "You can't leave now. The dining room is full."

"Then you'd better make a decision about Darla and Annie."

"I am *not* going to base all my decisions on what you and your daughter want. I still own the Dixieland Café, and I'll run it as I see fit."

"Okay, see ya," Flo said. She started for the door once more, with Patricia on her heels.

"Hey, fellow, I don't have all day. Either somebody waits on me now or I'm leaving."

"Okay, hold it!" Sam said. He turned to Annie. "Go wait on the gentleman. Give him anything he wants on the house." When Annie didn't so much as budge, he raked his hands through his hair. "What now?"

"In the future, when you tell me to do something, I would appreciate it if you said please."

"Please," Sam said between gritted teeth, wishing Buster had gone ahead and shot him the night before.

Annie left the kitchen with a fresh bandage on her finger and a smile on her face.

Relieved to have that problem out of the way, Sam turned to his kitchen employees. "Okay, Darla keeps her job, but this is absolutely the last time we settle matters this way. If you don't like one of my decisions, we talk it over, but the final decision is mine. I will not tolerate a mutiny. Understand?"

"You're the boss," Flo said, taking her time card and clocking in once more.

"That's right," Patricia agreed, doing the same. "We just work here, what do we know?"

Sam shook his head and started for the door, but Flo stopped him. "You really need to do something about that shiner, Sam. And please—" She paused and chuckled. "Puleese don't let anybody find out that some skinny gal gave it to you."

"Might not be a bad thing," Patricia said. "At least they'd forget about him being jilted."

Sam closed his eyes and shook his head. It just never ended.

It took Annie a good fifteen minutes to get the dining room under control again, but once she explained injuring herself, the customers were more than understanding and left good tips to boot. The teenagers dropped their forks twice more, forcing her to do her stoop-but-don't-let-them-see-up-my-skirt routine, before Sam sauntered over with clean ones.

"I see you boys are having difficulty holding on to your flatware," he said. "My waitress is busy with other tables and doesn't have time to keep fetching it like a golden retriever. Why don't you just motion for me next time your fork slips from the table."

"Are you asking us or telling us?" a lanky youngster with curly hair asked.

"I'm trying to come to a gentleman's agreement," Sam said smoothly. "My waitress has spent more time at this table than the others. I hope you'll remember that when it comes time to tip her."

"What happened to your eye, man?" another youth asked.

Sam placed his hands on the table and leaned forward. "One of my customers ticked me off. If you think I look bad, you should see him."

"Hey, we're cool," the curly-haired boy said, and the others nodded in agreement. "We're almost ready to leave anyway."

Sam smiled. "I'm glad we could have this little chat." He walked away.

Annie was taking an order at a booth nearby and couldn't help the small smile that lifted one corner of her mouth. Sam had taken up for her! Once the teen-agers left and she cleared the table, she saw six dollars in the center of the table.

By the time the last customer straggled out, Annie had cleared the tables and wiped down the counter and stools. She offered Sam a cup of coffee, but he declined.

"We need to talk," he said in a cool tone.

Something tightened in the pit of her stomach at the sound of his voice. He indicated a booth. "Have a seat." When she hesitated, he added, "Please."

Sam sat directly across from her. He measured her with a cool, appraising look. "Don't ever do that again," he said.

Annie studied him as well. She had already noted how good he looked in his navy sweater and khakis; up close she could see how the sweater set off his blue eyes. However, the two lines that ran across his brow told her he wasn't too pleased with her at the moment. "Don't ever do what?"

"Complain to my other employees about something I've done."

She look a deep breath. "I'm sorry, but I was bleeding, and I was upset. Flo wanted to know what was wrong."

"I make the rules here, Annie. I operate my businesses as I see fit. If you want to work here, you'll respect that."

She hitched her chin up. "You had no right to threaten Darla's job just because she's sick."

The lines deepened. "Darla is not sick. She's pouting so she can have her way. This is not the first time she's pulled something like this. But I shouldn't have to explain my reasons to you, now, should I?"

"I'm not trying to be difficult to get along with," she said, "but I've spent my entire life following someone else's rules. Whether I thought they were fair or not. I'm not going to make that mistake again."

Sam noted the stubborn tilt of her chin, and despite being annoyed with her, he had to admire her for the way she was taking charge of her life. He clasped his hands together and leaned closer. "Okay, here's the deal," he said. "You have a problem, you come to me. I'll be glad to discuss it, and I promise to be fair-minded. Agreed?"

She nodded. "That certainly sounds fair to me." Her eyes widened. "You mean I've got the job?"

"For the time being. I can't help but appreciate the fact that you came in at the last minute and all, and you didn't do nearly as bad as I thought you would."

"Gee, Sam, was that supposed to be a compliment?"

One corner of his mouth twitched. He almost smiled. "I'll need your Social Security number."

Annie scribbled it on a napkin and handed it to him. "How's your eye?"

"It hurts like hell. Why do you ask?"

'I've never punched anybody like that. You and your cousin scared me half to death."

"I didn't do anything. Buster acted alone."

"You could have said something. Instead, you let me make a complete fool out of myself."

Amusement flickered in his eyes. "I'm genuinely touched that you were willing to use your body as a shield to protect mine."

Annie's spine went ramrod stiff when she realized he was making fun of her again. Her mouth took an unpleasant twist. "Perhaps I acted rashly," she said in a grudging voice. "I probably should have grabbed Buster's pistol and shot you myself."

He almost laughed, but he feared she'd throw the napkin holder at him. Instead, he stood and walked to the door. "I have to check my messages across the street," he said. "Just in case somebody is looking for a good used car." He glanced over his shoulder. "I'll be back in time for the dinner rush. You'd better grab yourself something to eat while it's quiet. And stay away from sharp objects," he added, motioning toward her finger.

With growing frustration, Annie watched him cross the street to his car lot. She couldn't help but notice how good he looked, even from the back. He paused here and there to check on a car or wipe a smudge of dirt off a fender with the hem of his sweater, then he unlocked the construction trailer that served as his office. She shook her head, wondering if they would ever be able to spend time together without locking horns.

Annie went into the kitchen, where she found Flo reading the *Pinckney Gazette* and Patricia glancing through a Penney's catalog. She ordered a grilled-cheese sandwich, and they were quick to instruct her how to make it herself since they were taking a well-deserved break. She did so while peeking out front from time to time to make sure a customer hadn't appeared.

"You'll know if someone comes in," Flo said. "That bell over the door is loud enough so we can hear in the kitchen."

Annie made her sandwich and pulled a stool up to the long metal table, where they sat. Flo shared her newspaper with her. They sat in companionable silence until Annie finished her lunch and returned to the front. Several people came in for coffee and pie. Annie used her spare time to straighten up beneath the counter and sweep up. She came across a fall schedule for the community college and leafed through it. Classes had already started, but late registration was permitted for an extra fee.

Something stirred inside of her as she studied the courses offered in accounting, one thing she did happen to know something about. The classes began at eight A.M., she would have time to take a couple before she had to be at work, *if* she could get along with Sam Ballard well enough to keep her job.

If only she had a car.

Or even a bicycle, for that matter.

The bell on the door jangled and Lillian Calhoun

walked through the door. She gave Annie a big smile. "You got yourself a job! Good for you."

Annie smiled. "Yes, and I've done very well in tips for my first day."

Lillian offered her a high five. "I just stopped by to place a to-go order," she said. "What do you recommend?"

"The special tonight is chicken-fried steak, mashed potatoes, and green beans. Oh, and you get a small side salad with that."

"Sounds good." Lillian placed her order and Annie turned it in.

"Would you like a cup of coffee on the house while you wait?"

"I'd love it." Lillian reached for the community-college catalog. "What have we here?"

"Oh, I was just checking through the fall schedule and wishing I could sign up for a few of the courses."

"Why can't you? You could take morning classes."

"That's not the problem. The problem is, Darla lives way out in the boonies, and I don't have transportation. I could buy a bike, but it's quite a distance."

Lillian looked thoughtful. "Let's see. Kazue has an extra bike I bet she'd lend you, and my place is only a few blocks from the college and less than a mile from here." When Annie just stared at her, she went on. "I have a garage apartment. It's not bad, and the furniture's okay. Just needs sprucing up. You could rent it by the week if it would be easier on you, and I'd be willing to give you the first week free, if you'll clean it up."

"You would?" Annie asked. "You would actually do that for me?"

Lillian laughed. "Why wouldn't I? You would do the same for me if you could."

"Yes, of course." Annie realized she would indeed, and that made her feel pretty good about herself.

Lillian patted her hand. "That's what it's all about, honey. One hand scratches the other."

Flo slid a Styrofoam container into the window between the kitchen and dining room and Annie put it in a sack. But when Lillian pulled out her wallet to pay, Annie stopped her. "This one's on me," she said. "It's not much, but it's what I can do at the moment."

Lillian studied her as she tucked her wallet back into her purse. "You're going to be okay, Annie Hartford. Here's my card. It has my home address on it. Come by tomorrow and see the apartment. I think you'll like it."

Annie was still pondering those words long after Lillian left. Somebody believed in her! Somebody actually believed she was capable of doing anything she set her mind to.

There was only one problem. Money. She needed to sign up for the courses as soon as possible if she had any hopes of starting this semester, and there was no way she could hope to make enough in tips that quickly. She needed a temporary loan, and there was only one person she knew to go to.

She would ask Sam Ballard for the money.

FIVE

The dinner rush did not go well. Sam arrived back in time to assist Annie with the crowd, but she was so nervous having him there that she spilled or dropped almost everything she touched. A glass of iced tea slipped from her fingers and doused a truck driver sitting at the counter. He'd been flirting with Annie from the moment he walked in the door, but his smile faded abruptly as the cold beverage soaked the back of his shirt. Sam hurried over with a towel, and the three stood there looking at one another for a moment.

Annie batted her lashes at the customer. "Was that as good for you as it was me?"

Sam looked at her as though she'd lost her mind, but the trucker howled with laughter and ended up leaving her a five-dollar tip.

"What's wrong with you?" Sam asked, once he'd pulled her aside. "I feel like asking people if they have a good insurance policy before you wait on them. And all my profits are being eaten up by broken plates and glasses."

Annie wasn't about to confess that part of the problem was him. He watched her constantly, her every move. She didn't know if he expected her to run off with the money in the cash register or what. "I've never done this kind of work before, and this is my first day," she said. "Besides, you really need two waitresses to take care of this crowd. I'm doing the best I can."

He sighed. He knew she was trying, that she was also nervous, but the woman appeared to be the klutz from hell. It probably didn't help that every time she looked up she found him staring at her, which made her all the more nervous. But what did she expect? A man would have to be made of stone not to notice those legs and that tempting behind. No, he couldn't tell her all that and have her think he had no self-control. Besides, she was an employee, and he didn't get involved with women who worked for him.

"Let's just try to get through the night without seriously injuring anyone, okay?" he said.

Annie bit back the sarcastic reply that threatened to leave her lips; after all, she needed this job if she was going to get her life in order. And she needed a loan. So instead of mouthing off at him as he expected, she offered him a smile. "I appreciate you being patient with me, Mr. Ballard. I know I can do this job; I just need more practice. And I promise to pay for every single glass and plate I break."

Mr. Ballard? It was the last thing Sam expected to hear come out of her mouth. As Annie walked away he watched her warily. She was up to something.

By nine o'clock, all the customers were gone, and Annie's station was as clean as any hospital. Sam had cleared most of the tables; she didn't know if he was doing it to be helpful or if he feared she'd break more dishes. Flo and Patricia had already clocked out for the night.

Sam was at the cash register. "I'll buy your change if you like," he said.

"Oh, okay." Annie reached into her apron pocket and pulled out her tip money. "I'm afraid I only have a few dollars' worth of quarters here."

Sam was disappointed for her. She'd worked both the lunch and dinner shift, and all she had to show for it was a few lousy bucks. He glanced over his shoulder, an apology on his lips, then froze when he saw the mountain of bills in front of her. "Looks like you did okay."

"I think I did," Annie said. "I've got over a hundred dollars here. Oh, more than that. Is that good?"

Sam was stunned. Darla had hit that figure only a couple of times in the six years she'd worked at the restaurant, and that had been mainly on special occasions.

"That's damn good," he said.

"Especially when I told folks they didn't have to tip me to begin with," Annie said.

"You told your customers they didn't have to tip you?" He looked incredulous.

"That's right. I told them I was brand-new at being a waitress, that I was really just practicing, and that I would appreciate any pointers they could give me, but under no circumstances did I expect a tip. Well, they were so nice, they insisted."

Sam listened quietly, not knowing what to think about the woman. "I'm glad you did good," he said at last.

Annie cleared her throat. "While we're on the subject of money, I'd like to discuss the possibility of a small, short-term loan."

He arched one eyebrow. "You just cleared a hundred bucks in tips and you want a loan?"

"Yes, I need two hundred dollars." She reached into her pocket for a slip of paper. "I've got it all figured out. I'm willing to pay one point higher than the bank pays in interest, and I've scheduled my payments so that I'll have the debt paid off in three weeks. I'll probably be able to pay you back sooner, but I added the extra week just in case."

Sam reached for the paper. Surprisingly enough, she did have it all figured out, including the interest rate, late payments, and penalties. He shrugged. "Hell, Annie, I can just give you the money for as long as you need it. You don't have to go through all this. May I ask what you need it for?"

"I want to take a couple of courses at the community college. One in business and one in accounting. That is, if I can start a little late. I think I'd be pretty good at it."

He stood looking at her, his hands on his hips. "Do you know anything about accounting?"

Annie saw that he'd shoved the sleeves to his sweater up to his elbow. The dark hair on his arms was very manly. "I did some accounting work at the finishing school I attended."

His voice was a bit more friendly when he spoke. "I thought you were supposed to be learning how to fold napkins into fancy shapes."

"Oh, I can do that," Annie said, chuckling, as she reached for a cloth napkin and went to work. "But I had a problem with the dress code and curfews, so I stayed in hot water most of the time. The staff didn't want to send me home because my daddy was very generous where the school was concerned. I spent a lot of my spare time working in the offices. That's where I learned accounting."

"It's a good field to go into."

"I thought maybe if I did well enough, I might become a CPA."

Sam was thoughtful as he took in her determined look and stubborn chin. And she was a hard worker, even if she was the queen of accidents. There was more there than fluff, he decided. "Annie, I have a sneaking suspicion that you can do anything you set your mind to."

Annie felt her jaw drop. His words almost brought tears to her eyes. Other than Vera, nobody had ever really expressed a belief in her until she came to Pinckney. Now everybody seemed to think she was more than capable. "Thank you, Sam. I appreciate that. I sort of feel that way too."

He reached into his back pocket and pulled out his wallet, then fished out two hundred-dollar bills and slid them across the counter. "I don't charge interest to my employees and friends, and I don't need a repayment plan. You just pay me back when it's convenient."

She was genuinely touched and almost sorry she'd given him that black eye. "Thank you," she said. "Here, this is for you." She handed him the napkin, which she had managed to fold into a perfect rose.

"Wow," Sam said. "That's beautiful. What else can you do?"

She shrugged. "Oh, I can do all sorts of things with napkins. And I can make a poodle out of balloons."

They both laughed. For a moment they just gazed at each other in silence. "Well, I should finish closing up," he said.

"And I should go check on Darla. I called a couple of times today, but I didn't get an answer. Probably took the phone off the hook so she could sleep."

"Uh-huh." Sam looked doubtful.

"She really did look and sound terrible this morning, Sam."

"She'll be fully recovered by the time you get back. Take my word. I've known Darla a long time." He paused and looked thoughtful. "Which is why I don't have the slightest idea what the two of you have in common."

"Simple. She lent a helping hand when I needed it." Annie picked up her apron, folded her bills plus the two hundred dollars, and stuffed them into her pocket. "Do me a favor, Sam. Don't tell Darla how well I did tonight. I wouldn't want to . . . you know . . . hurt her feelings."

He gazed at her with a curious intensity. Finally, he shrugged. "It's really none of my business what either of you makes, Annie."

A new and unexpected warmth surged through her, and she almost wished she didn't have to leave. But she had been worried about Darla all day, and she wanted to make sure the woman was okay. "Well, good night, Sam."

"Good night, Annie."

She let herself out the door and headed for Darla's car. But as she drove, her thoughts of concern for Darla were interrupted by musings about Sam Ballard.

When Annie pulled into the driveway of Darla's mobile home, she was surprised to find the lights off, including the front one. She figured Darla must be sleeping. Luckily, she had the key; she groped for the door. One key slipped easily into the lock. She stepped inside the trailer and felt for the light switch.

"Hold it right there or I'll blow your head off," a male voice said, frightening Annie so badly, she thought her knees would collapse. The light came on, and she found herself facing the biggest man she'd ever seen. He had to be at least six-foot-six, with a barrel of a chest and thighs that made her think of tree trunks. His hair was jet-black, his jaw dark with stubble. In his arms was a shotgun.

"I'm not armed," she said, holding her hands over her head. "I have a little money. It's yours if you want it. Just leave and don't hurt us."

"*Me* leave?" he asked in disbelief. "Who the hell do you think you are telling *me* to get out of my own house?"

"Bo, who are you talking to?" a sleepy Darla asked, coming down the hall in her bathrobe. "Oh, hi, Annie, how'd your first day go?"

"You know this lady?" Bo asked.

"Bo, don't you even listen to anything I say? Annie's staying here till she can get on her feet. I got her a job at the Dixieland Café. Don't you recognize the uniform, numbskull?"

Annie watched him lower the shotgun, and she thought her bladder would give.

"Oh, yeah." A wide grin spread across his face as he grabbed her hand and pumped it furiously. "Nice to meet you, Annie. I'm Darla's husband, Boswell Jenkins. Bo, for short."

Annie looked at Darla. "I didn't know you were married."

"Actually, Bo's my *ex*-husband," Darla said. "They sent him to prison for writing bad checks and a few other nonessentials. I was so mad, I divorced him." She smiled. "But he's out for good, and he's promised to change his ways, so I've decided to take him back." She punched him in the chest playfully. "Big ol' goofball didn't even tell me they'd decided to let him out early."

Bo pulled Darla tight against him and kissed her hard. "That's because I wanted to surprise you, baby. And make sure nobody was warming my side of the bed while I was away."

"Bo, put that damn shotgun down before you scare poor Annie to death," Darla said, breaking free and putting her arm around the other woman. "How'd you do tonight? Make any good tips?"

Annie had to pry her tongue loose from the roof of her mouth in order to speak. "I did okay, I guess."

"I'm sure you did fine," Darla said. "And your tips will get better once you get the hang of things. Was Sam mad that I didn't show up?"

"A little at first, but he got over it quickly enough."

"How 'bout a cold beer, Annie?" Bo asked.

She was glad to see he'd put his weapon away. "No, I'd better not. Listen, Darla, you won't believe who offered to rent me her garage apartment today. Lillian Calhoun."

"No kidding?"

"She said I could move in tonight, as a matter of fact. It all happened so fast." She told Darla about wanting to sign up for classes at the college and how close Lillian's place would be to work and school. "I was hoping you wouldn't mind running me over to her place since I sort of promised I'd be there after work." It was a lie, and Annie hoped Lillian wouldn't mind her barging in at that hour, but she had no desire to spend the night at Darla's with Bo there.

"Are you sure that's what you want to do, honey?" Darla asked. "You know you're welcome here."

"I know, and you're very sweet to offer it to me, but I'd really like my own place. After living with my father most of my life, it'll be a special treat." She looked at Bo. "And I'm sure the two of you have a lot of catching up to do."

Darla and Bo exchanged a tender look. Finally, Darla turned to Annie. "I don't need to drive you to Lillian's. You can use my car as long as you pick me up in time for work tomorrow. Bo and I aren't going anywhere." She gave her ex-husband a coy smile.

Annie couldn't mask her relief. "Is it okay if I hang on to this uniform for a couple of days? Until I get one of my own?"

"Sure, honey. I'll even show you where you can buy one just like it in your size. Do you know how to get to

Lillian's place?" Annie was given brief directions before she was whisked out the door by an anxious Bo.

"I promise I won't try to shoot you next time you visit," he said, grinning.

She smiled. "Thank you." Annie hurried out to the car. She couldn't wait to get out of there, even if it meant sleeping in the backseat of Darla's junker.

Annie was on her way in minutes. One thing Darla had not taken into consideration when she'd given directions to Lillian's place was the fact that Annie knew absolutely nothing about Pinckney, or the landmarks that were supposed to help her find her way. It was after eleven o'clock by the time she found Lillian Calhoun's house. The place was pitch-dark, and the woman they called Diamond Lil had obviously tucked her jewels away and climbed into bed.

Annie pulled away from the curb and drove for a few minutes, wondering what she was going to do. She was dog-tired, and her eyelids were beginning to sag. She'd passed a motel, but it hadn't looked very appealing, and she was wondering if she crawled under the sheets whether she wouldn't find herself sharing space with some unwanted critters, when suddenly she found herself in front of the Dixieland Café. The lights were still on, and Sam was sitting at the counter doing book work. Thinking maybe he could give her the name and address of a decent hotel, Annie pulled into a parking space out front. Sam was obviously deep in thought, because he didn't look up until she knocked on the door. He glanced over his shoulder, then did a double take at the sight of her. He hurried to let her in.

"What's wrong?" he said quickly.

"May I come in?"

"Yeah, sure. Why aren't you at Darla's?"

Annie told him about Bo and her reasons for not wanting to stay. "I was hoping you might know of a nice motel."

"So, Bo Jenkins is out of the slammer, huh?"

She nodded. "Just got out today. Darla had no idea. I went by Lillian's house, but the place was dark. I didn't want to wake her."

"You don't have to stay in a motel," Sam said. "You can stay at my place."

"I beg your pardon?"

"Don't go giving me that look. I have a mean housekeeper. She'll protect you from me."

Annie sighed her relief. "Well, in that case. Are you sure you don't mind?"

"I wouldn't have invited you otherwise." He checked the clock over the cash register. "Damn, I didn't know it was so late. Do you want to follow me?"

Annie hesitated. "Sam, are you sure? I feel like I'm imposing. All I've done is rely on other people since I got here. I really wanted to be independent, you know?"

"Being independent doesn't mean you can't accept help when you're in a jam."

Annie regarded him. He appeared to be so strong and confident, she was certain he'd never had to ask for help. "Well, I appreciate it," she said.

"Don't mention it."

Their gazes met and locked and Annie felt a surge of warmth run through her that she was unprepared for. She glanced at the counter, where she saw a couple of ledgers as well as a stack of receipts and invoices. "What are you doing there?" she asked curiously.

"Book work. As usual I'm late filing my quarterly taxes."

"Why don't you hire someone to do it?"

"I just fired the best damn CPA in town because he screwed everything up. Which is why I'm in such a mess." He carried the books to the door, then balanced them on one hip while he unlocked it. "Maybe I'll hire you once you get your license," he added as he motioned for her to go through first.

She waited for him to lock up. "How many CPAs are there in Pinckney?" she asked.

"Two or three, I guess." He opened his Jeep and tossed the ledgers onto the front seat. "We can always use another one."

Annie followed Sam through town, in the opposite direction of where Darla lived. All the buildings and houses faded away until there was only blackness on either side of the car. Finally, he turned off the main road and drove down a long winding drive until he reached a two-story farmhouse that seemed to ramble on forever. Annie parked behind him in a circular drive where rose-bushes grew along a white fence.

The front door was opened almost immediately by an older woman in a bathrobe. She drew herself up and sniffed at the sight of Annie in her waitress uniform. "Well, Mr. Sam, what have we here?"

"Martha Fender, meet Annie Hartford from Atlanta. She'll be staying the night. I assume we have a guest room available."

"Yes, of course. She can stay in the yellow room at the back of the house. It has a nice view of the river."

"You're on the water?" Annie asked. When Sam nodded, she went on. "Can you fish in it?"

"Of course you can fish in it," Martha said. "It's plumb full of bass."

"I've never fished before," Annie confessed. "I've never even had a fishing license."

Sam and the housekeeper exchanged looks. Annie surprised the woman by taking both her hands in hers. "Miss Fender, I apologize for waking you in the middle of the night. I would never have inconvenienced you had I not been desperate."

Martha seemed to warm to her. "Could I fix y'all a snack?"

"I'll see to it," Sam told her. "Go back to bed, Martha. I'll make sure Annie gets settled in."

Martha nodded and disappeared down a back hall off the kitchen.

"She's nice," Annie said.

"She can be grouchy if the mood strikes her," Sam replied. "Are you hungry? I forgot to eat dinner tonight, and I didn't see you eat anything."

"I had one of the biscuits."

"That's hardly enough to keep you going. Have a seat at the counter, and I'll raid the fridge."

Annie did as he said, and while he pulled out packs of meat and cheese, she studied the kitchen. It was enormous, with white cabinets and wide plank floors that shone like a new car. An island sat in the center of the room with four comfortable stools. "How long have you lived here?" she asked.

Sam pulled out a jar of dill pickles and set them on the island. "All my life. The place belonged to my grandparents, then my parents. They raised cattle. Finally, it got to be too much for my folks, and they bought a place in town. They were just going to close the house because my father couldn't bear to sell it. So I took over."

"Do you still have cattle?"

"Oh, yeah. Not as many as I'd like, but my businesses keep me running."

"Do you own other property besides the restaurant and auto sales place?"

"I have a couple of convenience stores and a car wash. I mostly bought them as investments. If I could unload them at a good price, I would. And get rid of a few headaches too." He paused. "So, what do you want? Ham, salami, cheese?"

"I really don't expect you to wait on me, Sam. If you'll tell me where the glasses are, I'd like to pour myself a glass of milk." He pointed to a cabinet, and Annie went to it. "Would you care for something to drink?"

"Sure, I'll take some milk."

She grabbed the milk from the refrigerator and filled two glasses. Once she handed Sam his glass, she sipped her milk for a moment. "Mind if I look around?"

He'd finished making his sandwich and took a bite. "Make yourself at home."

Annie peeked into several rooms. A formal living room stretched across the front of the house. The wood floor was covered with wool floral rugs. A baby grand piano dominated the room, and the furniture was clearly of good quality without being ostentatious. The den was cozy, with its stone fireplace and overstuffed furniture in a navy, burgundy, and hunter-green plaid. An entertainment center took up one wall, boasting a big-screen TV and state-of-the-art CD player. Annie noted a laptop computer on the coffee table and wondered if Sam ever took time off.

"I like your place," she said, returning to the kitchen. "No wonder your father didn't want to sell it. But you're missing something."

He looked at her. "Like what?"

"A family. And a couple of big dogs."

"Don't even go there, Annie."

"You're going to let one bad experience affect the rest of your life?"

"Why should that concern you one way or the other?" he said tersely.

"Because I like to see people happy. And you're not happy."

He put his sandwich down. "You don't know that. You don't even know me. Besides, I'm very happy. And better than that, I'm not on the run."

Annie glanced down at the toe of her borrowed work shoes. "I suppose I am running. If it weren't for the kindness of others, I'd be sleeping in a homeless shelter tonight. And I wouldn't have a job or a cent to my name." She glanced around. "You seem to have everything you need. Why should I think you're unhappy?"

"You're not exactly destitute, Annie," he said, sarcasm slipping into his voice. "I know who your father is, and I know he's worth millions. I also know you're the apple of his eye."

"How do you know that?"

"I made a couple of calls."

She shot him a dark look. "You checked up on me?"

"Sheriff Hester wanted proof that you were who you said you were, and he wasn't about to back off. So I called my investigator friend in Atlanta and got the whole scoop on the Hartford family. My friend faxed me newspaper articles, pictures, you name it."

"I hope the sheriff is satisfied now that my privacy has been invaded," she said, none too happy with what she'd learned.

"You rode into town in a fancy limo that's worth no telling how much. Harry just wanted to make sure you came by it honestly. I thought I was helping you when I did what I did." He was quiet for a moment. "Want to know what Harry said when he found out you were the only heir to a vast fortune?"

"I can't wait," she muttered.

Sam chuckled. "He said you must be one angry lady to walk away from all that money. I told him you weren't angry, you were just standing up for yourself, and that no amount of money was worth giving up your dreams for."

Annie looked surprised. "You really said that?" When he nodded, she went on. "Gee, Sam, that was really nice of you to defend me."

He met her gaze. "I wasn't out to defend you, Annie. I was merely telling the truth. Honey, I been there and done that, and I know what it's all about. I pretty much made the same decision you made, which is why I'm not a married man today."

"I thought you were jilted."

His smile was derisive. "Folks have a habit of believing what they want to believe."

"So you allowed them to believe your fiancée dumped you and not the other way around?"

"Believe it or not, I do try to conduct myself with a little dignity. The only reason I'm telling you this is because I understand what you're going through."

"Have you ever regretted your decision?"

"No. Not even once. And neither will you." He put the sandwich meat away, then looked at her. "You're probably ready for bed. I'll show you where your room is."

Annie followed Sam up a flight of stairs and down a spacious hallway. He pointed to a closed door. "That's my room, in case you need something during the night." Two doors down, he led her inside a pale yellow bedroom with a pine sleigh bed covered with a beautiful comforter with a magnolia pattern that matched the drapes. A dainty settee and matching chair sat in front of the fireplace.

"This is gorgeous," Annie said.

"Lillian Calhoun decorated it," Sam told her. "I might let her do my room next. Well, good night." He turned for the door.

"Sam?"

He paused and looked at her.

"Thank you."

He stepped closer to her and gazed into her eyes for a moment. "You're going to be okay, Annie." Without stopping to think about it, he pressed his lips to her forehead. "You'll discover you have many friends in Pinckney." A moment later he was gone.

SIX

". . . so you see, I couldn't very well go through with it now, could I? I mean marriage is hard enough without marrying someone you don't love. Am I right?"

"You did the right thing, dear." Martha Fender sat across from Annie at the kitchen table, a pair of wire-framed glasses perched at the end of her nose as she let the hem out in Annie's uniform. Martha had tossed it in the washer while Annie showered, which explained why Annie was currently dressed in old bathrobe belonging to the housekeeper. "My father wanted me to marry a banker's son," Martha said, "but my heart belonged to a mechanic. We ended up eloping."

"How romantic," Annie said.

"We never had much when it came to material things, and I had to work all my life cleaning other folks' houses, but I wouldn't have changed a thing. We had three beautiful children and thirty-two years of happiness." She paused and looked up. "My Albert died of a sudden heart attack two years ago."

"I'm so sorry. I'll bet you miss him terribly."

"Oh, yes. Not an hour goes by that I don't think of him. And I thank the Lord that He gave me a good man. Not every woman is blessed to have a good helpmate by her side."

Annie sighed. "I've decided not to marry at all," she said.

"Oh, but dear, you're still young. You have your whole life before you. Don't you want children?"

"Yes, I've always wanted a big family. But I'm afraid it's just not in the cards for me, Mrs. Fender. That doesn't mean I can't adopt a child one day. But first I have to get my life in order."

In the next room, Sam tried to ignore the conversation and concentrate on the news program he was watching. But there was no ignoring Annie. He discovered right away that when she was around, his eyes and ears were fixed solely on her. He wasn't sure what that meant. Perhaps it was merely a mild attraction. No surprise there, since she was both bright and pretty. But there were parts of her personality that warmed him. Annie Hartford never met a stranger, it seemed. She'd already won over his moody housekeeper, simply by being herself.

"There now," Martha said, biting the thread and holding the uniform up for inspection. "You've got a good two inches."

"Thank you, Mrs. Fender," Annie said. "You don't know how relieved I am to have it. Why, I couldn't even bend over to wipe off a chair yesterday without fear of someone seeing up my skirt."

"I managed to let it out some too," Martha went on.

"That way you don't have to worry about busting out of it in the middle of the lunch shift."

Both women laughed as they pictured this in their minds.

"I'm glad you'll be moving into Lillian Calhoun's garage apartment," the woman said. "Not that Darla Jenkins isn't a sweet girl, mind you. But she's a little wild for my tastes."

"Well, it's hard to fault her knowing she's been alone for so long," Annie said. "Loneliness makes people do things they wouldn't normally do."

"I know all there is to know about being lonely," Martha said.

Annie touched her hand. "You don't ever have to be lonely again, Mrs. Fender. People may die, but the love never goes away, and that's what we cling to. See, I lost my mother as a young girl."

"Oh, you poor dear!"

Still sipping his coffee in silence, Sam perked up.

"But she's always been there for me. I kept her perfume in my room for a long time after she died. Once in a while, when I was missing her terribly, I would spray one of my bed pillows with her scent, and I could pretend she was visiting from heaven. Which was why I couldn't actually see her," she added. "But I knew she was right there with me."

Martha suddenly looked wistful. "I have wonderful memories of Albert." She suddenly chuckled. "You know, for someone who hasn't made a lot of decisions for herself, you sound very wise. You're going to do well for yourself, Annie. By the way, I'll be glad to come over and help you clean your new place."

"That's very sweet, but I doubt it's as bad as Lillian made it sound. I would like to invite you to dinner once I get settled."

"I'd love to come. But only if I can bring dessert. I make a wonderful sweet-potato pie. You just call me when you're ready for me to come see your little place."

Sam shook his head and took another sip of his coffee. Annie had the housekeeper eating out of her hand, for Pete's sake. What was it about the young woman that automatically drew people to her? He hoped she wasn't using them to get what she wanted. From what he knew of her father, the man had mastered that talent and amassed a fortune doing it. Once Annie got over her mad spell, once she proved to her father he could no longer push her around, she might call him to come get her. And if the man doted on his daughter as it was rumored, he'd waste no time getting there.

Annie Hartford was used to the good life. She would only carry trays and clean tables for so long before she began missing the mansions and her social life and the four-star restaurants and fancy cars. Once she got bored with this podunk town and the people in it, she'd high-tail it back to the big city and her sophisticated friends, and that would be that.

He was going to have to steer clear of Annie before he did something stupid.

Such as stare at her constantly in that short skirt until she became so self-conscious she dropped everything.

Such as invite her to sleep at his place because he wanted to spend time alone with her.

Such as think about her all the time because he hadn't been able to do much else since she'd hit town.

———◆———————◆———

"Oh, Lillian, it's absolutely adorable!"

"You really like it?"

The two women were standing in the living room of the apartment over the garage. Lillian had pulled the dustcovers from the furniture, and Annie was amazed that everything looked brand-new. A massive coffee table sat in the center of the room, piled high with books and magazines. "It's so cozy," she said. "I can imagine sitting in that antique rocker reading a good book."

"You don't think it's too froufrou?" Lillian said. "I decorated it for my mother when she came to live here several years ago. She absolutely refused to live in my house—said two women under one roof was one too many." She looked sad. "Then, last year, all of a sudden she was gone."

"Oh, I'm sorry," Annie said. "Was it a peaceful passing?"

Lillian looked at her, squinting her eyes as though they were unfocused. "Oh, no, she left in an RV. See, she met a retired stockbroker at the bingo parlor, and it was love at first sight. She crammed everything she could into one small suitcase, and they took off to see the country. I get postcards now and then. I expect to receive a wedding announcement one of these days."

"Well, that's wonderful. You must have a very youthful mother."

Lillian motioned to the large bay window at the front of the apartment. "Kazue made all the window treatments and bedspreads. There's one bedroom and a bath and a half. Plenty of room for one person."

"I love it," Annie said. "I'm prepared to pay you the first week's rent."

"No way. Our agreement was you'd get the first week free in exchange for cleaning it."

"But it's not dirty."

"Oh, it needs dusting and sweeping and mopping. I noticed some cobwebs in the bedroom."

"Cobwebs? Oh, my, that'll take me all of thirty seconds."

"And you'll want to scrub the bathrooms since they haven't been used in a while. You should find cleansers beneath the sink, as well as various supplies my mother left behind, most of them unopened. And there's a stackable washer and dryer in the storage closet just off the kitchen."

"Not that I'll be needing that right away," Annie said, laughing. "This is the only outfit I have to my name at the moment. I was wondering if there's a Salvation Army here, where I can pick up a few things till I can afford to shop."

"Honey, we can do better than that." Lillian checked her watch. "What time do you have to be at work?"

"Eleven-thirty."

"That gives us two hours. Let's go."

Annie followed Lillian out of the apartment and down the stairs. "Go ahead and get into my car, I'm just going to grab my purse and lock up."

They were on their way in minutes. Annie was delighted to see the small town in daylight. She smiled when they passed the community college. "I plan to enroll first thing in the morning," she told Lillian.

"Good for you. Kazue says you can use one of her bicycles for as long as you need it."

"I hope I don't run into problems because I have no identification," Annie said, remembering everything was in her purse in Atlanta. "Also, I'm enrolling late."

"Let me know if they give you a hard time in admissions," Lillian said. "As much money as I've given to that college, I expect them to cut my friends a little slack."

They arrived at the Second-Time-Around shop before long. Lillian parked her car. "Believe it or not, we have a few well-to-do ladies in Pinckney who wouldn't think of wearing the same outfit twice. They donate their clothes here because all the proceeds go to the women's shelter. I've heard you can buy an entire wardrobe for less than fifty dollars. I've never shopped here personally, you understand. I mean, the last thing I want is to run into one of those snooty old biddies from the ladies' club, wearing her linen suit. Know what I mean?" She chuckled. "I'd have to go out of town to wear them."

They stepped inside and a frumpy gray-haired woman smiled at them. "Oh, Lillian, I'm so glad you're back. You know that teal suit you were admiring on Marion Jones at the Christmas bazaar." She glanced around as if to make sure there was no one else in the shop. "She brought it in last week. Just five minutes after you left. And it's in A-one condition."

Lillian gave Annie a sheepish smile. "Well, I may have come in once or twice," she muttered out of the side of her mouth. "But we'll let that be our little secret."

A delighted Annie left the shop an hour later with two

pairs of jeans, several cotton shirts, and a lightweight jacket. She'd also picked up a couple of nightgowns, and a pair of sneakers that looked as though they'd come right off the rack. Lillian's almost new teal suit was folded and tucked into a paper sack.

"I'll have my seamstress sew teal satin on the collar and lapels, and Marion Jones will never suspect it's her suit," Lillian whispered as though afraid someone had bugged her car and would find out where she was doing her shopping these days.

Annie had already decided she would do her shopping at the secondhand store from now on. "I need to make one quick stop if you don't mind," she told her shopping partner. "I have to pick up socks and lingerie. And maybe a little makeup so I don't scare people."

"That's not likely to happen with your complexion, dear." Two minutes later they pulled in front of a Kmart. Annie hurried in to get what she needed while Lillian stepped into the book store next door. When they arrived home, Annie was touched to find Kazue had already dropped off a bicycle and left a nice note.

"Look, it has a large basket on the front," Annie said. "That'll be perfect for lugging books and groceries. If you see Kazue before I do, please tell her I said thank you."

Lillian smiled and nodded. "She's only too happy to help out; Kazue has had a tough time of it, too, what with her husband doing everything in his power to create problems with their divorce. Looks like you're all set, kiddo. I only see one problem. How do you plan to ride that bike in that short uniform?"

Annie chuckled. "I've already thought of that. I'll have

to wear my jeans and change clothes once I get to the café," she told Lillian. "Well, I'd better go inside and get ready for work. I'll put the bicycle in the trunk of Darla's car so I can ride home afterward."

Lillian started for her house, her bag tucked beneath her arm. "You have a nice day, hon, and don't work too hard."

Annie smiled, took several steps forward, and hugged the woman. Lillian looked surprised. "What was that for?"

"For being such a good friend to me, that's what. Thanks, Lillian."

Annie arrived at work wearing jeans and a cotton shirt. Her uniform and panty hose were tucked in a bag. Sam, who was sitting at the counter reading the newspaper, frowned. Here, he'd made all these promises about how he wouldn't gawk at the woman the way he had the day before, and she had to come in wearing a pair of behind-grabbing jeans that would have sent a preacher's blood boiling. "I hope you're not planning to wear—"

Annie disappeared into the rest room without a word. Five minutes later she came out ready for work. Darla almost bumped into her coming through the kitchen door.

"Well, hey there, missy. Who let the hem out of that uniform?" She winked. "How d'ya expect to make any tips in this joint?"

Annie looked thoughtful. "I suppose I'll have to rely on my excellent waitress skills. What do you think?"

"No comment," Sam said, and earned a dark look from the two of them. He stood. "I'm out of here."

"And not a moment too soon," Darla muttered.

"I heard that, Darla, and I'll remember it when it's time for your next raise."

"Raise? Did I hear someone say raise?" Darla glanced around as though trying to find the source. "I don't think that's a word we use very often in this place."

"I'd love to stay and chat," Sam replied, "but I've got a man coming in who wants to divorce his wife. Says all the woman does is nag. Imagine that."

Darla frowned at him. "I'm no lawyer, Sam Ballard, but that is not grounds for a divorce. Women were born to bitch and moan, and the only way to put an end to it is take them shopping."

"I'll remember to advise my client of that," he said.

Annie, who was filling saltshakers, chuckled. "And what exactly were men put on this earth to do?" she asked.

Sam turned to look at her, a thoughtful expression on his face. "We were put here to hunt for food, discover uncharted territories, and protect the weaker sex."

Darla threw a paper-towel roll, and he caught it. "Weaker sex, my foot!"

"I believe that's my cue to leave," he said, dropping the paper towels onto a nearby table and hurrying out the glass door. He managed to close it behind him before another roll hit the door.

Annie was still watching in amusement as Sam crossed the street to get to his office. She didn't hear Darla come up beside her.

"Well, well, we can't seem to take our pretty green eyes off of the man, can we?"

Annie blushed. "Nothing wrong with looking."

Darla nudged her. "You didn't spend the night with Lillian. I called first thing this morning, and she said you hadn't arrived yet."

The blush deepened. "It's a long story, and this place is going to fill up with customers any moment now."

"I'm not budging from this spot till I know, girl-friend."

"I stayed at Sam's."

"Aha!"

"His housekeeper was there. It was perfectly inno-cent."

"If you say so."

"The man doesn't even like me, for Pete's sake."

"Which explains why he can't take his eyes off of you."

"He watches me because he's afraid I'm going to break every plate in the house," Annie protested. She was thankful when three men walked through the door. Darla didn't make a move to go to them. "Are you going to wait on them or am I supposed to?" Annie asked.

"Why don't we take stations? I'll work the counter and booths, and you grab the tables. Then, tomorrow, we'll switch."

Annie grabbed three menus and hurried to the table. The restaurant filled up in no time, and although Annie stayed busy, it wasn't as hectic as the day before when she'd been the only waitress. Of course, Sam had helped, but it was much better having another waitress on the floor, even if it meant giving up a substantial amount of tips.

Once the rush had ended, Darla and Annie ordered a sandwich and cleaned the dining room as they went along. They ate in the kitchen and listened for the bell over the door.

"Did you tell Darla that Patricia and I saved her job yesterday?" Flo asked Annie.

Annie shook her head. She didn't particularly want to get involved in any more disputes. Unfortunately, Patricia didn't have that problem. She gave Darla a blow-by-blow account of what had occurred in her absence.

Darla looked genuinely touched. "Gee, I appreciate you guys sticking up for me like that. Sam can be such a pain sometimes. I don't think he'd really fire me, though. He's threatened to a number of times, but nothing ever comes of it."

"Well, you should a seen the way he was following around Miss Prissy yesterday," Flo said, motioning to Annie. "Cleaning off her tables, sweeping up after her, picking up broken dishes. And there were a lot of those." She rolled her eyes heavenward.

Darla laughed as the girl beside her looked embarrassed. "I was a real klutz yesterday," Annie confessed.

"That wasn't the reason he was following you," Flo said. "It was that short skirt."

"You never should've let the hem out of it," Darla told her. "Sam Ballard is considered the most eligible bachelor in Pinckney, Georgia."

"I don't think Sam has marriage on his mind," Annie said.

"You're probably right," Darla said. "The only thing he's interested in from a woman is a little action."

They all laughed. Flo choked on a biscuit, and Patricia came close to her performing the Heimlich on her, but couldn't do it right for laughing so hard herself. Once Flo caught her breath, she started laughing again, and the whole group fell into another fit of giggles.

"Excuse me, ladies," a male voice said. Sam Ballard was standing in the doorway wearing a frown. The women had been laughing so hard, they hadn't heard the bell over the door announcing an arrival. "There's a customer out front who would like pie and coffee."

"Oh, Lord!" Darla said, getting up right away. She hurried out the door with Sam on her heels while Annie cleaned up the remnants of their lunches. "That man takes life too seriously," Patricia said. "He needs to lighten up."

When Annie returned to the dining area, she found Sam sitting in a booth discussing business with a man and Darla filling sugar containers. Darla slid her a conspiratorial look, and Annie had to look away to keep from laughing. She wet a cloth and began wiping off seats. Sam and the man finished their business and shook hands.

"Great pecan pie," the man said to Darla. "Tastes just like what my mother used to bake."

"Why, thank you," she replied in a syrupy voice. "I baked it myself." Sam sighed and shook his head.

"No kidding?"

Darla fluttered her lashes at the customer. "I bake all the pies here."

"Wow." He looked at Sam. "You've got yourself a helluva waitress."

Sam nodded. "Yes. They threw away the mold when they made her."

"I'll bet you bake those biscuits too," the man said, leaning his elbows on the counter.

"As a matter of fact I do."

Sam walked over to Annie and cocked his head close. "This is when Darla does her best work," he whispered.

The corners of Annie's mouth twitched. "So I see." Even as she watched she couldn't help noticing how nice Sam smelled. His aftershave had a light musky scent that made her want to get closer.

"Note the body language," he said. "She's leaning slightly forward, chest thrown out, one hip thrust to the side. If I tried to do that; I'd end up in traction."

Annie giggled in spite of herself. Darla's eyes drifted toward them. She gave one wink and went back to her business.

"Note her tongue sliding in and out," Sam went on, "flitting across her full bottom lip. Keeping it moist. You know what the poor guy is thinking."

"She's quite good," Annie had to agree.

"Aha, he's reaching into his shirt pocket for his business card. Asking her to call him sometime."

Annie nodded. "He's pretty slick himself. Hope he doesn't have a wife and kids at home."

"And now the grand finale. He reaches into his back pocket for his wallet, takes out a bill. I'll bet you fifty cents it's a ten spot."

"No way," Annie said. "She's good, but after all, he only had pie and coffee. I'll say it's a five."

Darla took the money and tucked it in her apron pocket, and the smile she gave almost had the poor man tripping over his own feet as he made his way out the door.

"What'd he leave you?" Sam said.

Darla looked offended. "A waitress never discusses her tips."

"Annie and I have money riding on it."

"So do me and Patricia," Flo said, leaning in the order window. "And I do not appreciate you telling him you made the biscuits. I should make you split that tip with us."

Darla gave Sam and Annie a coy smile. "I'll give you a hint as to what he tipped me. The man on front of the bill invented the lightbulb."

Sam sighed heavily. "Thomas Edison invented the lightbulb, Darla. He's not pictured on any currency."

Darla shrugged.

He held his hand out to Annie. "We both know Hamilton is on the ten-dollar bill. You owe me fifty cents, Miss Hartford."

Annie dropped two quarters into his open palm and went back to work.

SEVEN

It was after nine o'clock by the time Annie clocked out, changed into her jeans, and said good night to everyone. Although Darla offered to take her home, Annie assured her she would be fine as she took her bike from the trunk of her friend's car.

The streets were lit up with old-fashioned lampposts, which made it easy for Annie to find her way. It took less than ten minutes to reach Lillian's house, but Annie passed it by, having decided she would go to the grocery store and pick up a few items. The basket would easily hold two grocery sacks.

Sam knew he had no business following Annie home. For one thing, she was an adult, perfectly capable of finding her way. Secondly, she was taking a safe route. She would not be traveling down back roads or dark alleys, and only a complete imbecile would accost her right on Main Street, one of the most heavily patrolled areas in town.

So why the hell was he following her?

Not that he wasn't enjoying watching that perfect tush, each time she raised slightly off her seat to pedal harder. He was tempted to get closer but didn't for fear of being discovered. Finally, disgusted with himself for what he was doing, he slowed and turned on his blinker. He needed to go home and stop thinking about Annie Hartford. But just before he was to turn, he saw her pass Lillian Calhoun's house altogether. Sam frowned. Where was she going? He turned off his blinker and drove on.

Annie pulled into the Piggly Wiggly supermarket some minutes later and attached her bike to a metal stand with the plastic-coated metal strap and combination lock Kazue had provided, along with the combination to unlock it. She went inside the store, grabbed a shopping basket, and immediately forgot about the limited space in her basket. Upon checking out, she discovered she had four sacks of groceries.

No sweat, she thought. She'd just have to stack 'em high and ride back very slow.

From across the parking lot, Sam watched Annie come out of the store with a cart filled with groceries. He frowned. Now, how the hell did she expect to get all those bags into the basket on her bike? He sighed. Women did the damnedest things sometimes.

Annie positioned her cart beside the bike, opened the lock, then straddled the bike and began loading the sacks into the basket. By the time she put the fourth bag in, she was having serious doubts as to whether she'd be able to get home with them. What had she been thinking when she'd put so many items in her cart?

Annie turned the bike around, aiming it for home. With a sigh for good luck, she climbed on and began to pedal. She could feel every heavy item she'd purchased—the half gallon of milk, a large box of laundry detergent, two whole frying chickens because they'd been on sale, not to mention the large pack of hamburger meat that she planned to divide and wrap for the freezer.

And a whole lot more.

She struggled to keep the bike upright, but it wasn't easy considering that she was on a hill. No wonder the trip to the store had been so easy. She vaguely remembered coasting down the incline. Annie muttered a few curse words under her breath as she fought the basket and tried to keep pedaling at the same time. The front of the bike had a tendency to pull left. She decided she must've put most of the heavier items on that side.

She didn't even hear the pickup truck come up behind her, but when her bike drifted toward the center of the road, the driver laid on his horn, scaring her half to death. The front wheel veered far left, and Annie tried to right it, then overcorrected. All at once she lost control. The bicycle went down; she and her groceries went with it, then skidded down the hill some twenty feet before coming to a stop. She winced as her right knee and elbow scraped asphalt and her foot twisted painfully. When she glanced up, she found a mess; cans rolling down the hill, eggs broken with the yellow oozing from the carton. A can of soda pop spewed in her face.

Suddenly a car screeched to a halt. Annie looked up

and saw Sam Ballard standing over her. "I'll be generous and give you an eight-point-five on that fall."

Annie blinked back tears of frustration and embarrassment. "Very funny, Sam." He got down on his haunches, and even though she was hurting, Annie had to admit he had very nice haunches. That made her all the more angry.

"Are you hurt?" he asked, his tone becoming serious.

"Just my pride," she said. "And a couple of scrapes." She was thankful there was little to no traffic.

"Do you think anything's broken?" She shook her head. "Okay, why don't I help you to my car, and you sit tight while I try to chase down your canned goods."

"All of my bags are torn."

"I've got some bags in my backseat I've been meaning to take to the recycling center." Using great care, he pulled her into a standing position and supported her as she limped to his car. "Are you sure you're okay?" he said.

"My ankle is killing me. I hope I didn't break it." She knew she would never be able to work if she'd fractured it.

"No, it's not broken," Sam assured her. "You wouldn't be walking if it was." He managed to put her in the front seat, grabbed several bags from the back, and went about picking up groceries. A car filled with teenagers flew by, and he yelled for them to slow it down. "I'm afraid those kids ran over your box of cereal," he told her as he set the bag on the back floor.

It took some time, but Sam finally managed to gather up the groceries, even the busted eggs. Once he'd loaded all the bags into his car, he put the bicycle in back and drove toward Annie's apartment. He parked out front, climbed out of the car, and hurried around to her side. "You got your house key handy?" he asked.

She handed it to him. He dropped it in his shirt pocket, then, without warning, scooped her high in his arms. She protested. "You're injured," he said, "and you probably have a sprained ankle. You don't need to be on your feet."

"But I'm too heavy," she said as he carried her up the stairs with an ease that surprised her.

"Damn right you are. What do you weigh, about one-eighty?"

She gave him a sour look, but he paid her no mind as he paused to unlock her door. He carried her inside, glanced around, and set her down on a chair, propping her leg on a matching ottoman. Her jeans were torn at the knee. He ripped them farther.

"Hey, these are my good jeans," she cried.

"Shut up and let me see how bad it is. Man, this is bad!"

Annie leaned forward. "How bad?"

"I might have to amputate."

She slapped his hand away and took a look for herself. Her right kneecap was badly scraped. "Oh, great!" she muttered sarcastically. "Just what I need."

"You're going to be a real siren in that short uniform," he muttered, reaching to untie her sneaker. "I may have to fire you." He tugged her sneaker off.

"Ouch!" She jerked her foot away as pain shot through her ankle and radiated up her calf.

"I have to take a look at it, Annie," he told her. "Now try to be brave. Remember, you'll probably bear children one day. You might as well get used to dealing with pain."

"What do you know about giving birth?" she said derisively.

"Are you kidding? You wouldn't believe the stories I hear from other guys whose wives have gone through it. Now, try taking a few deep breaths to keep your mind off it."

"I don't believe this. I've got a sprained ankle, and you're teaching me Lamaze techniques." Nevertheless, she groaned and carried on as he gently pulled her sock free.

"Hmm," Sam said.

"Does he have all his toes and fingers?" Annie asked, noting that, despite the pain, Sam's hands felt very nice on her.

"Yes, but he's definitely on the plump side."

"It's sprained, isn't it?" she asked, afraid to look.

"Hard to say. Is it normally black-and-blue and puffed up like a blowfish?"

She leaned forward once more, noting her anklebone was now hidden beneath a bulge. "Oh no. What am I going to do now?"

"First we have to treat your wounds," he said. "Do you have a first-aid kit?"

"I don't think so. But the woman who lived here before me left a bunch of stuff in the medicine cabinet. She sort of left in a rush," she added, remembering what Lillian had told her about her mother.

"Okay, let me check." Sam disappeared down the hall. When he returned, he had an armful of medical supplies. "You lucked out, Annie Fay," he said. "This woman must've worked for the Red Cross."

"My name is not Annie Fay," she said.

An easygoing smile played at the corners of his mouth. "Yeah, but it fits, don't you think?"

"Absolutely not! I'm not Annie Fay or Annie Mae or Annie Jo. I'm just plain Annie."

"Nothing plain about you, Miss Hartford," he said, kneeling before her.

"Oh really?" she said, trying to remain casual and indifferent to his comment. But her fingers were tense as she clasped them together in her lap. Had he just flirted with her or was she imagining things? She struggled with the uncertainty that he'd aroused in her, and when he glanced up at her, she felt impaled by his gaze. They both froze, stunned by conflicting emotions.

A shadow of annoyance touched Sam's face, and he looked away quickly. What was he doing giving this woman goo-goo eyes when they had absolutely nothing in common and couldn't be in a room together five minutes without getting on each other's last nerve? Besides, it was only a matter of time before Annie went traipsing home with her tail tucked between her legs. In a week she would have tired of hamburger and chicken, and she'd return to her champagne-and-caviar lifestyle. His look was hard as he regarded her. "We're going to have to get you out of those jeans," he said.

"Is that the best you can do to get a woman out of her clothes?"

"Listen, honey, I don't have to resort to chicanery to get a woman out of her clothes. I've discovered most are only too happy to oblige."

"Oh, brother!" Annie laughed. "You have one inflated ego for a small-town man, but I should warn you, you've met your match this time. Now, if you'll help me up, I'll try to get these off."

"What, here?"

"Unless you're embarrassed by the sight of a woman in her silk boxers."

He sighed. "Okay, but I liked it better when women wore bikini underwear."

"Your kind would."

Sam ignored the jab as he helped her to a standing position. "Try to put all your weight on your left foot," he said, when she yelped at the pain in her ankle.

"Easy for you to say."

"Put your hands on my shoulders for balance."

Annie did as he said. She felt him reach for the fastening on her jeans. Her stomach did a nosedive. "What are you doing?"

"I'm helping you out of your jeans."

"Shouldn't we dim the lights and put on soft music first?"

He unzipped her. "I'm acting in a purely clinical way; I assure you." What a crock, he told himself. "Okay, I'm going to slide them down. I'll try not to hurt you." He tugged the jeans past her hips and felt his gut tense when he spied her silk boxers. They were short, flesh-colored, and the sexiest thing he'd ever seen. Her thighs were creamy smooth and well toned. "You can sit down now," he said.

Annie wondered at the sudden hoarseness in his voice as he lowered her into the chair. He sat on the ottoman and worked slowly getting the right leg of her jeans past her knee without causing her more pain. Annie flinched a couple of times as the fabric brushed the wound.

"You skinned it pretty good," he said, then leaned closer to study the cut. "It's not deep enough to require stitches."

"My right elbow hurts," she said, shrugging out of her jacket. Sam checked it.

"You scraped it. You're probably going to be bruised, kiddo. I'm afraid you're no longer the perfect female specimen." He reached for the bottle of peroxide he'd found, as well as a bag of cotton balls. He cleaned her injuries as gently as he could. "I'm not sure what this is," he said, holding up a brown bottle, "but it says it heals and protects." He applied it to her knee, and Annie yelped.

"It burns," she cried, unable to sit still. "Blow on it."

Sam did as she said, but it wasn't easy while laughing at her antics. She glared at him. "Stop being a big baby," he told her in a stern voice.

"Why don't you put that stuff on yourself?" she snapped.

"I don't have any wounds."

"I can do something about that. Get me a knife."

"That's no way to talk after all I've done to help you," he said, a teasing light in his eyes. He reached for a clean but well-used Ace bandage, wrapped her ankle tightly, and fastened it with safety pins, since he hadn't found any metal clamps. "Well, that's the best I can do until I receive my medical degree."

"Thank you, Dr. Sam."

"Don't mention it. Just do me a favor. Next time you need groceries, call me, and I'll either drive you to the store or let you use my car." He gathered the medical supplies, including the used cotton balls, and carried them down the short hall to her bathroom. When he came back, he found Annie smiling. "What's so funny?"

"Nothing. I was just going to invite you to have ice cream with me, that's all."

"Sure. You want me—" He stopped abruptly. "Oh, damn, the container is sitting on the backseat in my car, isn't it?" He hurried out the door to his car and grabbed as many bags as he could. He knew which one held the ice cream because it had leaked through the paper sack onto his seat. "Damn," he muttered again, and hurried up the steps. He tossed the ice cream, bag and all, into her freezer, grabbed a wet cloth, and went back down to his car. Once he'd cleaned up as much as he could, he gathered up the rest of the bags. Upstairs, Annie was hopping toward the kitchen on her left foot. She was a sight to behold, the silk boxers revealing long, shapely legs. She wasn't the least bit self-conscious in her skimpy state of dress.

"What do you think you're doing?" he said, his eyes fastened to her behind.

"Getting our ice cream."

He followed her into the cozy kitchen and pointed to the table. "Sit," he ordered. "I'll get our ice cream as soon as I put away your refrigerated items."

"Stop bossing me around," she said, but did as he told her—not because she felt she had to obey his command, but because her foot and ankle were throbbing something fierce. She sat in one of the chairs and propped her foot on another.

"You're a stubborn little cuss, you know that?" Sam

said, putting her milk and orange juice in the refrigerator. He looked in another bag. "Hmm, I suppose you want these sanitary napkins and feminine deodorant spray in the bathroom." He shot her a disarming smile that she chose to ignore. "Ah, yes, here's pink disposable razors, toothpaste and mouthwash, and what's this, *acne* cream?" He looked at her. "You don't have acne."

Her look was deadpan. "That must mean it's working. Why don't you just stick it all in one bag, and I'll put it away later."

"You bought a Mickey Mouse toothbrush?" he said in disbelief.

"It was half price. I'm trying to learn to conserve my money."

"That explains this day-old bread. Is it worth eating stale bread just to save a few cents?"

"Sam, would you just put my refrigerated items away and leave the rest?" Annie said. "I don't need a running commentary on everything I bought from the grocery store."

"You shouldn't be eating all this junk food, Annie," he said, holding up a bag of potato chips and another of mini–candy bars. Do you know how much fat is in this stuff?"

She was more than a little peeved. "Do I look like I need to be on a diet?"

"Maybe not now. But you keep eating this stuff, and ten years from now you won't be able to get through the front door."

"Perhaps that would be a good time to have this discussion," she said coolly. "If we're still speaking in ten years."

He shrugged. "Okay, forget I said anything. You probably have this great metabolism that the rest of us lack."

"As a matter of fact, I do. Which is a good thing for me since I hate dieting and exercise with a passion. I learned a long time ago I'd rather be a size ten or twelve than live off bean sprouts so I can be a size six. Now, would you kindly serve dessert?"

He reached into the freezer and pulled the bag out that held her butter-pecan ice cream. He opened the container. " 'Fraid we'll have to drink it, Annie Fay. This stuff is no longer in solid form." He checked the cabinet, found two glasses, and filled them with the thick liquid. He carried them to the table, along with spoons and napkins.

Annie went to work on hers right away, fishing out chunks of pecans. Sam watched with amusement. He'd managed only to sip half of his by the time she finished.

Annie dropped her spoon into her glass and held her head with both hands. "Oh no, my head hurts."

He chuckled. "That's what you get for eating it so fast, you little pig." He shoved his glass aside.

"Aren't you going to finish that?"

"I'm not big on sweets. My weakness is Patricia's biscuits."

"Mind if I have it?"

He set his glass in front of her. "Go for it. Slowly this time, so you don't give yourself an ice-cream hangover."

Annie started on his. "I don't think I'm going to be able to work tomorrow," she said.

"I pretty much figured that one out on my own."

She sighed. "I had planned to register for the fall semester tomorrow." She groaned and pushed the glass aside.

He stood and picked up their glasses, then carried them to the sink to rinse. "I can drive you over in the morning if you like."

"Would you?"

"I may even have a pair of crutches in my attic at home from when I tore a ligament in my leg a few years back while running in a race. I'll have to adjust them, of course, since you're such a runt."

"I really appreciate it, Sam. And I won't forget. In fact, as soon as I can get around a little better, I'm going to cook dinner for you. What do you think of that?"

"You know how to cook?"

She hesitated briefly. "Of course I know how to cook."

He noted the pause and almost smiled. She probably couldn't cook a meal if her life depended on it. "Yeah, I'd love to have dinner. It's been a while since I've had a good home-cooked meal."

"Doesn't Mrs. Fender cook?"

"Huh? Oh, not often. She's getting up in age, you know. So I'll look forward to dining with you, Annie." His gaze dropped to her legs and grazed a path down one shapely calf to her bandaged foot and ankle. "Now, why don't I help you and Mickey Mouse to the bathroom so you can brush your teeth before bed."

Annie didn't argue. She stood, and he scooped her up once more, stopping by the counter so she could grab her toothbrush. He set her down before the bathroom sink and waited outside the door while she readied herself for bed. Finally, she opened the door. "I can hop the rest of the way," she said.

"What time do you want to be at the college tomorrow?" he asked.

"What time is good for you?"

"How's eight o'clock?"

"That's fine. I'll have to take a shower, and that means coming out of this Ace bandage."

"Try to stay off your foot as much as possible, okay? It's not going to heal if you keep putting weight on it."

"Yes, sir."

"Okay, I'll stop telling you what to do. You're going to do what you want anyway." He grinned and tweaked her nose. "I like those silk boxers, Annie."

She gave him a smug smile. "I know. You haven't taken your eyes off them all night."

"Know what you're problem is, Miss Hartford?" he said. "You're too cocky for your own good. One of these days—" He paused and shook his head.

"What?"

"One of these days, you're going to meet a man who's going to show you how unnecessary all that nonsense is."

"Yeah, yeah, yeah." But as Annie watched him go she wondered if she hadn't already met him. It was indeed an interesting motion, especially since she'd always prided herself on having full control over what few relationships she'd experienced.

Sam was the kind of man who would expect a woman to give all she had, no holding back. And he would take all he could, even as he delved deeper.

A shiver ran up her spine as she considered it.

Annie was almost asleep when the phone on the nightstand rang, startling her. She snatched it up. It was Darla.

"How'd you get this number?" Annie asked her. "I didn't even know I had phone service."

"I used to play bingo with Lillian's mother," Darla said. "I just took a chance on calling, didn't know if the phone had been disconnected or not. But I wanted to check on you. Sam called and told me about your ankle. Are you in pain?"

"Not unless I do something stupid like try to walk on it. I'm just sorry that I can't come in tomorrow. I hate leaving you in a lurch."

"Hey, I can handle it. Just as long as you can walk by the time the Okra Festival starts."

"I should be okay by then," Annie told her.

"I have another reason for calling," Darla said. "Bo and I've talked about it, and we've decided to remarry."

"Oh, Darla, that's wonderful!" Annie said, wanting to sound happy for her friend.

"We want to do this at the Okra Festival. I've already contacted the people in charge, and they said we could do it Sunday afternoon on the courthouse lawn. They think it'll be great publicity; they're even going to have the band play the "Wedding March" for us. And guess what, Annie? I'm going to wear your bridal gown."

"How romantic!"

"It has to be slightly altered and hemmed. I hope you don't mind."

"Why should I mind? I gave that dress to you. You may do with it what you wish."

"Bo asked Sam to be his best man not more than ten minutes ago, and I'd like for you to be my maid of honor."

Annie was more than a little surprised at the request. She and Darla had only known each other a couple of days. "Oh, Darla, I'm touched," Annie said. "But surely you have a best friend—"

"She got married and moved to Ohio a year ago," Darla said. "Now she's expecting a baby in two weeks and can't travel. What d'you say? Will you stand up with me?"

"Of course I will. I'd be honored." Annie was already wondering where she would find a dress.

As if reading her mind, Darla brought it up. "You can go through my closet and choose anything you want to wear," she said.

"Uh, that's okay," she said. "I want to buy something special for the occasion."

"Whatever you say, honey. Well, I'd better go. Bo is calling me from the other room."

Annie hung up the telephone and lay there for a moment, wondering where she was going to find a dress for Darla's wedding. Perhaps she'd call the secondhand store and ask the owner to check and see if she had something suitable in her size for an afternoon wedding.

It amazed her that she'd been in town only a few days and she already had a network of friends. Her father would never approve of Darla and Bo, of that she was certain, and he would find the ladies of the Pinckney Social Club quite laughable.

Annie didn't care. Winston Hartford had chosen her friends all her life, and she was now in a position to choose her own. She might not have a whole lot in common with Bo and Darla, but the other woman had been good to her and that's what mattered. Her father could keep his opinions to himself.

And she would tell him that when she saw him, because she knew, sooner or later, he'd show up on her doorstep, demanding to know what the hell she thought she was doing.

It was just a matter of time.

EIGHT

Sam showed up shortly before eight the following morning wearing jeans, a starched plaid shirt, and a rust-colored blazer. He was bearing crutches. "Here, try them out," he told Annie.

She reached for the crutches, but her attention was drawn to Sam's clean-shaven face and clear blue eyes. His hair, though neat and conservatively cut, was full and fell naturally about his head. She realized she'd been wanting to touch it since the first time she'd laid eyes on him. Annie tried the crutches and was surprised they were the perfect height. "How'd you know?" she asked.

"Just a wild guess." He saw that she was dressed casually in jeans and a cotton blouse—she looked like a fresh-faced student; nobody would've believed she was pushing thirty. Nor would they have guessed she was worth a lot of bucks. He supposed that's one of the things he liked about her. She wasn't the least bit pretentious. "How does the ankle feel this morning?" he asked.

Annie tucked her money into the pocket of her jeans. "Much better. I'm hoping by tomorrow I'll be able to work."

"Don't rush it," he said. "No sense taking a chance of injuring it further. I'd rather you stay off it as much as possible so you can work during the Okra Festival."

"There's only one problem with that," she said. "What am I supposed to do for money?"

"We can work something out. Ready to go?"

"I don't want to put myself further in debt to you," she said, struggling to get through the door with her crutches.

Sam locked up, then took the stairs ahead of her, thinking he could break the fall if she slipped.

"I'm not very fast," she admitted.

He watched her hobble down the flight of steps at a snail's pace, but there was a look of determination about her. "You know, I could carry you down much quicker," he said.

"Yes, you probably could, if I let you."

"Why are you so stubborn?"

"I like doing things for myself." She looked up at him and grinned. "Besides, I know it drives you crazy when I won't let you take charge."

"Oh, dear, what happened to your foot?" a woman's voice said.

Annie followed the sound. Lillian was obviously on her way out, because she was dressed in a smart business suit, and her diamonds were all in place. "I fell off Kazue's bicycle last night," Annie said.

"Oh, my goodness!" The woman came closer. "Is it broken?"

"It's just a sprain, thank goodness. Skinned my knees and elbows too. Real attractive stuff, if I may say so."

"Why didn't you call me?" she demanded.

"Sam saw the accident and rushed me home," Annie replied. "Luckily, your mother left some medical supplies behind, including this Ace bandage."

"You're lucky you didn't break something," Lillian said, then glanced at Sam. "I'm glad you were around to help. I hope you're taking her to the doctor."

"It's much better this morning," Annie assured her. "Sam's giving me a lift to the college so I can register. I can't afford to waste another day."

"I spoke with the director of admissions last night," Lillian said. "They'll work with you."

They said good-bye, and Sam helped Annie into the passenger seat of his car. It took only a few minutes to reach the college. Sam parked as close to the main doors as he could get, then helped Annie out. "Go on in," he said, holding the door open so she could pass through. "I'm going to park the car."

Annie entered the building and hobbled toward a set of double doors marked ADMISSIONS. A tall, angular woman in an old-fashioned beehive hairdo greeted her.

"My name is Annie Hartford and—"

"Say no more," the woman told her. "Lillian Calhoun has already called." She reached for the catalog. "Which classes were you interested in taking?"

Annie thumbed through the pages and pointed them out. The woman checked her wristwatch.

"Oh, my, the accounting course begins in ten minutes. Since you've already missed the first two classes, I strongly suggest you try to make this one. You can purchase your book and whatever supplies you need in our bookstore across the hall. Why don't you go ahead and take care of that, and I'll complete your registration form."

Annie ran into Sam in the hall and explained the situation. He entered the bookstore with her and together they found the two books she needed, as well as a pad of paper and some pencils. Back in the office, Annie scribbled her address and phone number, signed the necessary forms, and was pronounced ready. The woman at the counter gave her directions to her first class, and Annie thanked her and stepped out in the hall with Sam.

"Whew, that was fast. I wasn't planning to start today," she said, feeling a bit anxious.

"No better time than the present," he said. "When do you expect to be finished?"

"The classes are back-to-back. I'll be out by ten-thirty."

"You've got everything you need?"

"I think so."

He stood there looking at her, feeling as though he should do more. "Well, at least let me carry your books to your first class, Miss Hartford."

"Why, thank you, Mr. Ballard." She chuckled.

"What?"

"I feel fifteen again. I can't believe I'm actually going back to school to learn something I can use in the real world."

He smiled. "Personally, I was a little impressed with your napkin-folding abilities. You'll probably forget all that cute stuff once you become a bona fide CPA."

"I'm counting on it," she told him.

They'd reached the door to her classroom. "Don't be nervous," he said.

"Easy for you to say." They stepped aside as a group of students paused outside the door. They couldn't have been more than eighteen or nineteen. "I'll probably be the oldest one in the room," Annie whispered.

As if acting on cue, a white-haired man approached the door. He glanced at them curiously before going inside. "Maybe not," Sam said.

"Well—" Annie raised her eyes to his, and their gazes locked. "I suppose I'd better go in." But she realized she had no desire to leave Sam at the moment.

"Okay, listen," he said quickly. "I'll pick you up outside your second class. We can grab an early lunch afterward if you like."

Annie's smile was sincere. "Thank you, Sam." Without stopping to think about it, she leaned forward and kissed him on the cheek. He smiled and opened the door for her, then tucked her books beneath one arm.

The walk from the door to the teacher's desk was a long one for Annie, not because of the crutches but because all her insecurities sprang to life the minute she entered the classroom. She could feel everyone's eyes on her, hear her father's voice telling her she had no business trying to educate herself. She was not part of the working class, he'd told her more than once. Her job was to marry well and be an asset to her husband. Annie had always considered his beliefs archaic, but she'd never had the nerve to do anything about it. Until now.

Mr. Barnwell, the white-haired man, who was also the instructor, accepted her admissions slip and told her to sit wherever she would be most comfortable.

"You're behind by two chapters, Miss Hartford," he said. "You shouldn't have any trouble catching up. If you have questions, you can discuss them with me after class."

Annie smiled and thanked him. Class began. At some point she realized she was so engrossed in the lesson that she was no longer nervous.

Sam was waiting outside Annie's second class when she came out. A good-looking young man was carrying her books for her. He paused at the sight of Sam. "Nelson, you can just give the books to my cousin," Annie said sweetly.

The boy did as he was told, nodding at Sam quickly before returning his attention to Annie. "Will you be okay getting home?" he asked.

"Oh, yes. Sam will take care of me from here on out. But I appreciate all your help. You certainly made my first day a lot easier."

"No problem," he said. "Hey, I'll see you around, okay?" He smiled and walked away.

Sam wore a dark scowl. "Cousin?" he said. "Since when?"

Annie blushed. "I didn't want Nelson to think there was anything between us."

"Obviously."

Sam started down the hall ahead of her. He wasn't sure why he was so annoyed, only that he was. Annie tried her best to catch up with him so she could explain. "Hey, you don't owe me an explanation," he snapped. "I certainly wouldn't want to cramp your style, what with you surrounded by all these young studs."

"Sam, I was just having a little fun with you, that's all.

If it was in bad taste, I apologize. You know I don't have any interest in these so-called young studs."

"You could have fooled me by the way you were looking at that guy."

"That guy just happens to be a kid and way too young for me."

"He certainly didn't seem to notice."

"I don't know what more I can say, other than I'm sorry. I don't know why you should care one way or the other. Face it, you don't even like me most of the time." They had reached the main door leading out. Sam held one open so she could exit. Annie was glad to see his car parked beside the curb. Without a word, he opened it for her.

They rode in silence. When Sam passed her apartment, Annie didn't bother to inquire where they were going, since he'd invited her to lunch. A few minutes later he parked in front of the Dixieland Café. "We're having lunch here?" she asked.

"You have a problem with that?"

"Of course not."

Sam climbed out of the car and helped her out of the passenger's side. He walked beside her to the front door and opened it.

She came to an abrupt halt at the sight of Darla holding a cake with candles. Lillian, Kazue, Inge, and Cheryl stood on either side. "Surprise!" they cried out.

"What's this for?" Annie said.

"Your first day of class," Darla said.

"And for taking charge of your life," Lillian told her.

"Sam, did you know about this?" Annie asked. She

turned, but there was no Sam. She caught sight of his taillights before he pulled out of the parking lot.

Sam knew he had not acted wisely by walking out on Annie's little party, but he had not been in the mood for socializing after what had happened at the college. As he sat in his office, glowering, he kept an eye on his restaurant. Who the hell did she think she was introducing him as her cousin? And him standing there panting like a dog as he waited for her class to end, thrilled to death that she would let him carry her books and drive her home.

Damn idiot. That's what he was.

Well, maybe that's how she felt. Perhaps she wasn't attracted to him. If that was the case, he had no business sniffing around her back door. The door to the Dixieland Café opened, and Lillian stepped out, holding it open so Annie could exit with her crutches. Kazue and Inge followed behind and helped her into Lillian's car.

That meant he didn't have to run her home. Good. He had better things to do with his time. A pickup truck pulled onto his car lot, and a couple got out. Sam watched them, trying to decide if they were looking for a lawyer or a good used car. Finally, they made their way to a newer-model truck sitting on the front row. Sam shrugged out of his jacket, rolled up his shirtsleeves, and went to work.

Annie sipped a cup of coffee from her chair as she rested her sore ankle on the matching ottoman. She was depressed, despite the little party that had been given in her honor. Lillian had insisted on showing the girls the apartment, and they all declared it was the cutest thing they'd ever seen. But Annie, feeling bad about what had happened between her and Sam, took small pleasure in their excitement. Cheryl was quick to notice how quiet she was, and she insisted they leave so Annie could rest her ankle.

She felt miserable about hurting Sam's feelings in what was supposed to be a simple joke and nothing more, something he obviously hadn't found a bit funny. Her apology hadn't seemed to matter one way or the other. The fact that it had bothered him so much made her wonder what was going on between them. Had she mistaken his kindness for friendship when there was more to it?

Boy, was she confused. Was this the Sam Ballard who had made it clear from the beginning that he wasn't looking for a relationship? Had things changed, and had she somehow missed it?

A knock at the door made her jump. She put her coffee cup aside, pushed herself up, and hobbled to the door. She checked the peephole and saw Sam. She unlocked the door and threw it open, ready with an apology. He didn't give her a chance. He stepped inside, kicked the door shut, and pulled her into his arms roughly.

Sam saw the small O of surprise on Annie's lips and took it as an invitation. He captured her mouth with his and kissed her hard, sending his tongue deep inside. The kiss was urgent and demanding as he crushed her to him. When he finally released her and backed away, he had to steady her to keep her from falling. He saw the disbelief in her eyes as he raked her body with his gaze.

"Would your cousin kiss you like that?" he demanded. Without waiting for an answer, he swung around and slammed out the door.

Annie stood there, feeling as though she'd been punched in the chest.

NINE

Annie awoke early the next morning to a chilly apartment. She grabbed a blanket from the closet and wrapped it around her, made coffee, then hit the books. She was surprised at how much she already knew. She supposed she owed it to that fancy finishing school and her habit of not coming in on time. She was so engrossed in her studies that she didn't realize it was time for lunch until someone knocked on her door. Lillian had arrived bearing finger sandwiches and a large shopping bag.

"It's chicken salad," she said. "I had to make a tray for the garden club." She looked down at Annie's bandaged ankle. "How's it doing?"

Annie suddenly realized she was starving. She reached for one of the sandwiches and bit into it. "Mmm, this is great. My ankle is a lot better. I've tried to stay off of it as much as possible. Sit down."

"I can't stay but a minute." She sat down. "Guess where I've been?" she whispered. "The secondhand store. I was cleaning out my closet, and I took a load up. Look what all I found in your size." She offered her the bag.

Annie looked inside and saw that it was crammed full of clothes—jeans, a nice pair of slacks, some blouses, and a couple of sweaters. "Oh, Lillian, thank you so much for picking these up. How much do I owe you?"

"Don't be silly. I could buy a potted plant for what that cost me."

"I don't want you buying my clothes, Lillian."

"Okay, then buy me a potted plant when you can afford it. But I wanted to tell you, they have several lovely dresses that you can wear to Darla's wedding. I thought you should go look for yourself. I don't mind taking you when you're ready." She looked around. "Are you comfortable here, dear?"

"Very. I'm afraid I haven't done much cleaning due to my accident. But you know as well as I do the place was spotless."

Lillian nodded, then was quiet for a moment as she studied Annie. "Well? Aren't you going to tell me what's going on with you and Sam?"

Annie felt her face grow warm. "He's been very kind to me since I hurt myself," she said.

"And?"

Annie chuckled. "And that's all I have to report at this time, Barbara Walters."

Lillian smiled. "You know, there are a lot of women in this town who would love to sink their claws into that man. Hell, he owns half the town. He's probably worth more than any of us know." She paused and rolled her eyes heavenward. "But why am I telling *you* that? You've got more money than all of us put together."

"Correction. My father has a lot of money. It's very possible he's disinherited me after what I did." Annie shrugged. "I don't care. Money has never held much importance with me."

"That's because you've never had to rake and scrape for it, hon."

"That's true. But I sort of like knowing I can take care of myself. It's a little scary, of course. I certainly hope I can go back to work soon."

"Dear, nobody in this town is going to let you go hungry or homeless. That's just the way we are."

"So I've noticed. It's so refreshing to live in a small town," Annie said. "And one day, when my new friends need a good accountant, I hope they'll come to me, because I'm going to give them a special deal."

"I know you will. And you'll have plenty of business, believe me. Earl Burnsed has been my accountant for some thirty years now. He was old when I first hired him. I have no idea why he keeps practicing. Folks say he's so old, he farts graveyard dust."

Annie laughed so hard that she almost choked on her sandwich. Lillian hurried into the kitchen for a canned soda. "Now, the other reasons I stopped by—" She paused and smiled. "It has to do with Darla's wedding. You know we're all just crazy about her. Well, I thought it would be fun to throw her a little bachelorette party. Invite only those who are real close to her, maybe six or eight of us total. What do you think?"

Annie nodded enthusiastically. "What a great idea.

But let me have it here, Lillian. After all, Darla has done so much for me."

Lillian looked around. "I suppose this place is big enough for that many people. Now, I plan to supply the food and drinks, so you needn't worry about any of that."

"When are you thinking of having it?"

"We've no time to waste. Once the Okra Festival begins, the two of you will be too busy. Is tomorrow night too soon? Say six o'clock?"

Annie thought about it. That would give her time to straighten the place. "That's fine," she said.

They spent twenty minutes discussing the party. "How am I going to get Darla over here?" Annie asked.

Lillian pondered the problem. "Well, she knows you're on crutches, right?"

Annie nodded. "She's called a couple of times."

"Okay, you call her and tell her—" She grinned. "Tell her you've fallen and you can't get up." They both laughed. "One more thing," Lillian said, "and you can't tell anybody. Not even the others." She leaned close and whispered. "I've hired a male stripper."

Annie's eyes almost popped out of her head. "No way."

Lillian blushed. "Yes. He's just a kid, but he looks good in blue jeans, so I have to assume he'll look just as good in a thong."

Annie shook her head, but she was more than a little amused. "Oh, Lillian, you are so bad."

The women jumped when someone knocked on the door. "Remember, not a word to anybody," Lillian said, getting up. "If Darla catches wind of it, it'll ruin the whole surprise."

"Cross my heart," Annie said.

Lillian opened the door. "Oh, hello, Sam. I see you brought lunch."

Sam stepped inside, looking a little self-conscious with Lillian there. "Hi," he said, then noticed the plate of sandwiches. "I see I'm a little late," he said, obviously disappointed.

"Oh no!" Lillian protested, "I just this minute brought these over. Annie hasn't had time to eat one yet." She winked at Annie as she picked up the plate. "I'll just put these in the refrigerator, and you can have them for dinner. How's that?"

Annie, who'd been stuffing finger sandwiches in her mouth since Lillian arrived, merely nodded. "I'm starving," she lied to Sam. "What'd you bring me?"

"Well, I didn't know what you'd like, so I got you a foot-long hot dog, large fries, and a milkshake."

"That sounds yummy," Lillian said, patting Annie on the back and giving her a devilish smile.

"Why don't you stay and split it with me?" Annie suggested.

"Oh, I have to be on my way, dear. Besides, you need to eat. You're a bit on the skinny side, if you ask me." She turned to Sam. "Don't you think Annie's a bit on the skinny side?"

"Yes, she could use a little more meat on her bones. Uh, don't let me run you off," Sam added.

"You're not doing anything of the kind," Lillian said. "I'm cleaning out my attic this afternoon. Have to run a bunch of old clothes over to the shop before it closes. To help the needy, you understand." She looked at Annie. "Enjoy your lunch."

When Lillian was gone, Sam glanced around. "Have I missed something? I feel very confused."

"No, we were just discussing Darla's wedding and what we plan to wear," Annie said. "You know, girl stuff. Please—" She motioned to a chair.

Sam sat down and began pulling food out of the sack. He didn't notice the dubious look on Annie's face as he shoved the hot dog and fries in front of her. "I probably should have called first," he said. "But I was afraid you wouldn't have lunch with me after last night." He looked at her. "I'm sorry about what happened, Annie. I don't know what came over me. Guy stuff, I guess." He gave her a sheepish smile.

"It's okay. I never meant to embarrass you when I said what I did at school. I was just teasing. The last thing I want to do is offend you."

"Why?"

She met his gaze. "Well, you've been very kind the past couple of days. If it weren't for you—"

"Forget all that," he said, sliding his chair closer to her. "I would've stopped and helped anyone in your predicament that night. But that's not why I took you to school and carried your books and helped plan that little surprise party."

"You had a hand in that?"

"Of course."

"As I said before, why?"

He leaned forward and put his hand on her knee. "Because, Annie Hartford, I'm so damned attracted to you, I can't think straight. In fact, I'm crazy about you. I don't know any other way to tell you than just to blurt it right out."

Annie scratched her head. "I don't know what to say."

"You don't have to say anything. I wanted you to know why I did what I did." He sighed. "I know what you're thinking. You're thinking it's too soon, but believe me, I know my own mind. That's one thing you don't have to worry about with me. I'm very stable, and I don't hand out lines to women. I don't have to."

She smiled. "So I hear."

He shrugged. "I'm a normal healthy male, what can I say? But I'm up-front with women, and I'm cautious as hell. I've never fathered a baby, and I'm free of disease. I like women, but I've only been in love once. I'm not even sure it was love, maybe just a serious case in infatuation. Hell, I was only twenty-five at the time, so who knows?"

Annie shook her head. "Sam, why are you telling me all this?"

"I want you to know what kind of man I am, Annie. Just in case you think you might be attracted to me too. I'm sorry, I'm keeping you from eating your lunch. You must be starving."

Annie looked down at all the food and thought she might gag. "I think I'll eat this later," she said. "You've given me so much to think about."

"I've upset you."

"No, nothing like that. I just can't eat with all this on my mind. Once I settle down, I'll be able to eat the whole thing. Trust me."

"You know, come to think of it, I'm not very hungry either. How's your ankle, by the way?"

"Much better. I should be able to work on Monday." She paused for a moment. "Sam, I hate to pry into someone's life, but what do you know about Darla's ex-husband, Bo?"

He shrugged. "I've known him all my life. Went to school with him, as a matter of fact. We were both on the football team. He and Darla married right after graduation. After a few years he opened a building supply store, and Darla helped him run it.

"Was it a good marriage?"

Sam nodded. "Oh, yeah. Those two were made for each other. They bought a house and a piece of land, and Darla planted fresh vegetables and flowers. They seemed very happy. Until Darla decided she wanted to start a family. Bo was all for it. When it didn't happen, Darla consulted a specialist and discovered she couldn't have children. That's when the trouble started."

"What kind of trouble?"

"Bo stopped coming home. Said Darla wasn't easy to live with in those days. He'd stay out all night in the bars, playing video poker machines. He got into debt pretty bad."

"That's when he began writing bad checks?"

"That's not all he did. He got into shoplifting. He'd sell the goods for money so he could try to pay back his debts. He got caught big time, and they shipped him off."

"Do you think he's a changed man after all he's been through?"

"Oh, yeah. Bo has absolutely no desire to go back to prison."

"I don't want to see Darla make a mistake," Annie told him.

"Don't worry. Bo is stable and levelheaded, and he's always been a hard worker. He just got sidetracked."

"Well, I hope things work out for them this time."

Sam nodded. "Oh, before I forget—" He reached into his back pocket and brought out a small sack. "I stopped by the drugstore and got you this. It's an ankle sock. See, it's made out of an Ace bandage, only it fits over your heel and ankle, and it's a lot less bulky."

She was touched. "Thank you, Sam. This will be a lot more attractive too."

"Honey, you would be attractive in a burlap sack." He leaned close and kissed her lightly on the lips. "So what do you think?"

"About the sock?"

"About us, silly. Do I stand a chance?"

Annie gazed into his eyes. He was sincere. She was tempted to confess she felt much the same, but she didn't. She didn't want to rush into anything. After all, she had to get her life in order. "Yes," she said softly. "You definitely have a chance."

"Then, how about a picnic tomorrow at my place? We can even go fishing if you like."

"Picnic?" The thought of sharing an afternoon with him almost made her giddy. Then she remembered the party. "What time were you thinking of having it?"

"Around one o'clock. I'll get Martha to cook some of her fried chicken. It's not as good as Flo's, but it's close."

"I'd love to," Annie said. "I just can't stay late because I have so much studying to do." She wasn't thinking about studying. She had to clean her apartment for Darla's party.

"I could help you study," Sam said, giving her a suggestive wink.

She laughed. "Forget it. Besides, if you knew that much about accounting, you wouldn't be complaining all the time about having to do it."

"I shouldn't have to do it," he said. "But the CPA I was using is so old that—"

"I've already heard," Annie said, laughing at the thought. "Perhaps it's time Pinckney had a young, female CPA."

"Yeah, but where are we ever going to find someone like that?"

Annie smacked his arm playfully. "Watch it, Ballard. There may come a time when you need me to do your books. I'd hate to have to charge you more than my other friends."

"Perhaps by then we'll be more than friends." It sounded good, he told himself, but he knew he'd already crossed the friendship line and wanted more. He was falling for Annie Hartford fast and hard. And although he knew there was a chemical attraction between them, he was certain what he was feeling went much deeper than that.

"You're being presumptuous, Mr. Ballard," Annie said. "I have not checked out all other handsome eligible bachelors in town."

"They're all spoken for," he said quickly. "All of them are happily married. I'm all that's left."

"Oh? How sad for you that nobody wanted you." She clucked her tongue.

There was a wicked gleam in his blue eyes. "Oh, they wanted me," he said. "But I run pretty fast."

"I should warn you. If you should decide to run from me, I won't chase you. I've never chased a man in my life."

He picked up her hand and kissed her open palm. "I'm not going to run from you, Annie. That's the last thing you have to worry about." Sam checked his wristwatch. "I have to go. Somebody's coming in to talk to me about doing their will and to look at a used van I have on the lot. And the ice machine is down at the restaurant. I've been meaning to replace it for a couple of years." He sighed heavily.

"Sam, you're too busy to have a girlfriend," Annie said laughingly.

"I'm going to unload some things, Annie. I'm tired of running myself ragged. And I'm never too busy for you." He kissed her, started for the door, then backtracked and kissed her again.

This time the kiss was slow and thorough, his tongue tracing her full bottom lip and sending Annie's stomach into a wild swirl. She kissed him back hungrily, sliding her fingers through that sexy head of hair that had beckoned her touch from the beginning.

When Sam raised his head, he was breathing heavily. "I could get used to kissing you," he said. "How about I pick you up shortly before one tomorrow, and we can pick up where we left off."

She could still taste his lips on hers. "I'll be waiting," she said, noticing her voice had dropped an octave since he'd first gotten there.

Annie spent the remainder of the day studying and

washing the clothes Lillian had purchased for her. And daydreaming about Sam Ballard. Although she was determined to get through chapter three of her *Fundamentals of Accounting* textbook, her concentration was shot after the sweet kisses she'd shared with Sam. She thought about closing her books and cleaning, then decided it was in her best interest to stay off her ankle for at least one more day. She didn't need to have problems with the Okra Festival set to begin. She could clean the next day after the picnic; in the meantime she would pull herself together and concentrate on schoolwork.

Yeah, right. Sam had only to waltz in through the front door and her brain turned to sawdust. She needed to put things into perspective. Just because they were attracted to each other didn't mean they were meant to be together.

Darla called as Annie was getting ready for bed. "Just checking to see how you're doing, kiddo."

Annie was about to tell her how much better her ankle was, then remembered she was supposed to call Darla the next day and pretend she was having problems. "I think I may have overdone it today," she said. "I gave this place a thorough cleaning and—"

"Annie, why would you go and do something like that?" Darla demanded. "You know better. I would have come over and helped you before work this morning if you'd called me."

"I'm going to take it easy tomorrow," she promised.

"Well, let's hope so. I'm going to need your help when the Okra Festival hits town, and they're already setting up for it."

"How are the wedding plans coming along?"

"There's not much to do. Sam called me last night and offered to give a small reception at his place. I thought that was very nice of him. And the gown is being hemmed and altered a bit. Hope you don't mind."

"We've already been through this, Darla. It's your dress, do what you want."

"Guess what?" Darla said, changing the subject. "Bo has already found a job working for a builder."

"That's good news," Annie told her.

"He's always been ambitious, but, well, he screwed up, and the rest is history. I just hope folks don't look down their noses at him."

"Everybody deserves a second chance," Annie said.

"So you're going to stay off that ankle?" Darla asked, changing the subject abruptly. "Don't make me come over there and smack you."

"Yes, Mother." She paused. "Darla?"

"Hmm?"

"You're going to make a beautiful bride."

"So are you, honey."

"I'm never getting married."

"Yeah, yeah, yeah. I've seen the way a certain gentleman looks at you. He's sworn off marriage too." She chuckled. "I'm going to enjoy watching the two of you eat your words."

"That's never going to happen," Annie told her in earnest.

"We'll see."

Darla hung up, leaving Annie to ponder the conversation.

TEN

Sam picked up Annie shortly before one and drove her out to his place. "So what did you do all day yesterday?" he asked, helping her out of his Jeep.

"Studied."

"All day?"

"Most of it. I was surprised how much of the material I know."

"Well, now that you kept your nose to the grindstone yesterday, you can play today."

"I intend to." Annie's ankle was no longer sore, and she took great pleasure in walking his property and listening to funny tales about his childhood. The night had brought with it an early cold snap, and Annie was glad she'd worn a sweater. She thought Sam looked sexy in an off-white sweater and jeans. As she stood on a bolder and watched the sunlight shimmer on the narrow river that ran behind Sam's house, she felt him slide his arms around her waist. He nipped the back of her neck playfully, and she shivered.

"Watch it, Ballard," she said. "That kind of stuff drives me wild."

"Really? What else drives you wild?"

"Wouldn't you like to know."

"Yes, as a matter of fact, I would. What does it take to find out."

She faced him. "No way. A girl has to have a few secrets."

"I like mysterious women."

Annie gazed into his eyes. They seemed even more brilliant in the afternoon sunshine. She reached up and touched his jaw, raised her fingers to his cheek. He smelled of soap and aftershave. He smiled.

"What's the smile for?" she asked.

"You want me to kiss you, don't you?"

She blushed and pulled her hand away, but he put it back. "What makes you say that?"

"I can tell. You have that look."

"Look?"

"You want me."

She laughed, but she could feel the blush spreading. "Oh, I do, do I?"

"It's written all over your pretty little face, Annie. You want me so badly, you can't stand it."

"Oh, good grief!" She pulled away and started to walk off, but he grasped her around the waist and squeezed her tight while she shrieked.

"Admit it, Hartford. You want my body. You've wanted it since you first laid eyes on me. Well, guess what?"

Annie struggled to break free but couldn't. Laughter bubbled out of her. "What?"

"I'm yours, baby."

She felt something in her stomach dip. He turned her around in his arms and gazed down at her face. She tried to look serious, but it was difficult. "I don't want to rush you, Sam."

"Rush me, Annie. Please."

"What? And have you think I'm just like all the other women who don't think twice about taking advantage of a vulnerable man. No, Sam. I'll only end up breaking your heart the way I did poor Eldon's."

"I'll risk it."

"Besides, I'm far too sophisticated for you. Remember, I'm a big-city girl, and you're just a country bumpkin."

His smile was mischievous. "Oh, Annie, you are really asking for it. I will show you no mercy when the time comes."

"*When* the time comes? You're mighty sure of yourself, aren't you? You should be saying *if* the time comes."

His look turned serious. "Oh, it's going to happen. The only question in my mind is when and where. This could be a good time for you to start thinking about it." He kissed her, then, without warning, scooped her high and carried her to a group of Adirondack chairs. He placed her in one. "Give your ankle a rest, pretty lady. I'm going inside to grab our picnic lunch. I'll be right back."

Annie watched him walk away, his stance tall and straight. He seemed to have full confidence that they going to be lovers, and while the thought was certainly appealing, Annie couldn't help feeling jittery about it. Not that she understood what there was to be afraid about. She was very attracted to Sam, had been from the beginning. What woman wouldn't welcome him to her bed?

But then what? Where would they go from there?

Annie was still thinking about it when Sam returned with a large picnic basket and blanket. "Let's walk closer to the river," he said. "There's sort of a beach down there."

Some minutes later they were sitting on the blanket and Sam was pulling all kinds of goodies from the basket, many of them placed in plastic containers. There was fried chicken, potato salad, deviled eggs, a plate of different cheeses, and another of corn muffins. Sam pulled out two bottles of root beer and opened them.

"This looks delicious," Annie said. "I'll have to thank Martha for going to so much trouble."

"I helped," Sam said. "I sliced all this cheese."

"Oh, my. A man who cooks."

He filled her plate. "It wasn't easy, missy. I almost cut my finger on the cheese slicer."

"You are a very brave man, Sam. Very brave."

"You really think so?" he asked, offering her the plate. "'Cause there's nothing I wouldn't do to protect you." He sighed. "Damn, I'm getting so goofy over you, there's not much I wouldn't do to impress you."

"No kidding? Would you take your clothes off and dive in that cold river?"

He arched one brow. "You can't stop thinking about getting me out of my clothes, can you?" He saw the pink on her cheeks and laughed. "Yes, I would swim that raging river for you, Annie Hartford. And when they pull my frozen body from it, everyone would say I died for a good cause. Anything else?"

She laughed at the game they were playing. "Would you purposely hit your thumb with a hammer as hard as you could?"

"I would consider it an honor, darlin'."

"Step in front of an eighteen-wheeler traveling seventy miles per hour?"

"For you? In a heartbeat."

"Give yourself a paper cut?" she asked, chuckling.

He frowned. "Hold it right there, Annie. You've gone way too far." He cocked his head to the side. "What would you do for me?"

She was thoughtful. "The ultimate sacrifice, Sam. I'd eat canned spinach for you." She shuddered at the thought. "The whole can if I had to."

"No way."

"Yes, Sam. Only for you."

"I'm one lucky guy."

"Yes, very."

Once they finished their lunch, Annie closed the containers and wrapped their used plates and flatware in a large dish towel. Sam lay down on the blanket, pulling Annie against his chest. They stared at the cloudless blue sky. She didn't know how long he talked, but the sound of his voice lulled her into a sense of well-being that she hadn't felt in many months. She snuggled closer to him, and her eyelids fluttered closed as his voice seemed to come from far away.

Sometime later Sam shook her. "Annie, wake up, you're trembling."

She opened her eyes, blinking as she tried to remember where she was. She was cold. She sat up and pushed her hair from her face. "I must've dozed off. What time is it?"

"Four o'clock."

"What?" She almost shrieked the word and pushed herself into a standing position. "I have to go home," she said.

He looked surprised. "Now?"

"Right this minute."

"What's the hurry?"

"Huh? Oh, I still have a lot of studying to do before class tomorrow."

"But you said you studied all day yesterday."

"Yes, but I'm behind because I started late."

"And you said you knew most of the material. What gives, Annie? I was going to make us a cup of coffee and build a fire. You haven't even had dessert."

He was still sitting on the blanket as if he had no intention of moving. "Look, Sam, I had a wonderful afternoon, but I have to go and that's all there is to it. Maybe we can do this some other time, okay?"

His shrug was noncommittal. He stood, grabbed the blanket and basket, and started for the house. "Do I have time to drop this off?"

"Sure. I'll wait for you in the Jeep."

Annie was already settled in the passenger's seat with her seat belt on when Sam climbed in. He looked at her. "Did I do or say something to offend you?"

"Of course not. I just have things to do." It would have been easier telling him the truth, that she was hosting Darla's bachelorette party, but Lillian had sworn her to secrecy.

"Anything I can help you with?"

"No."

They made the drive in silence. Annie figured she'd have little more than an hour to dust and vacuum the place and change clothes. She unbuckled her seat belt and had her hand on the door handle as Sam pulled into the driveway. She wasted no time climbing out. "Thanks, Sam, I had a great time."

He reached for his own door. "Wait a minute, I'll walk you up."

"No!" She tried to calm herself. "Don't bother," she said. "I can manage perfectly."

He shrugged, but his jaw was tense. "Fine."

Annie hurried up the stairs without a backward glance. She would explain it to him later. She unlocked the door and stepped inside. She headed for the kitchen, opened the door, and chuckled when she found several large bottles of wine. Lillian had also dropped off a half-dozen platters of hors d'oeuvres. Quickly, Annie went to work, first cleaning the half bath in the hall, then dusting the place. She wiped down the counters and ran a wet mop over the floor. She vacuumed the main rooms and decided it was enough.

The guests arrived promptly at six. "We all rode together and hid the car," Kazue said.

Another knock and Lillian walked in. "Is everybody here?" she asked Annie.

"Not quite," she said, winking at Lillian to let her know the stripper hadn't yet arrived. "Should I go ahead and call Darla?"

"No, let's give it a few more minutes."

Sam had driven all over town, just trying to gather his thoughts. He was one confused man. One minute Annie acted as if she was having the time of her life; the next thing he knew, she couldn't wait to be rid of him. If he lived to be one hundred years old, he would never understand women. Perhaps he was rushing her; after all, they'd known each other less than a week, and much of that time had been spent locking horns. But he, a man who'd never believed in love at first sight, had known from the minute he'd looked into those green eyes that he wanted her. He supposed that's why he'd fought the attraction so hard. And he still wanted her. He didn't care that her life was in a mess right now, he would gladly help her any way he could.

The thought that Annie might not feel the same about him was crushing. She'd told him he had a chance with her, and she'd responded when he'd kissed her. But if she wanted more time, he had no choice but to oblige her. He would take her to school and pick her up. He'd wine and dine her and send fresh flowers, and he would become more tolerant of her as a waitress. What did it matter if he lost a few plates now and then? He'd just buy more.

Having come to a decision about his relationship with Annie, Sam wanted to run it by her and hopefully try to find out what had happened to sour the afternoon. But as he started to turn in to the driveway leading to her apartment, he saw a young man park in front of Lillian's house and make his way up the driveway.

Sam recognized him immediately, even though he was

dressed differently than before. He wore a tux that was so tight, it was indecent. The shirt was open to his navel, revealing a wide chest covered with brown hair. Why was he carrying a boom box? Sam wondered.

Sam felt his gut clench as he watched the man climb the stairs to Annie's apartment. No wonder she'd been in such a hurry to leave. He could just imagine what kind of studying the two had in mind. A man didn't go out wearing a tux like that unless he had something on his mind. Sam gritted his teeth as he considered what Annie might wear to complement the man's outfit. A G-string? He ground his back molars together until it hurt, then drove away.

When Annie answered the door, her jaw dropped open at the sight of the man on the other side. "Nelson, is that you?"

He grinned. "Hi, Annie."

"Do you two know each other?" Lillian asked.

Nelson kissed Lillian on the cheek. "Annie and I have a couple of classes together."

"Oh, how nice," Lillian said. She turned to Annie. "Nelson's mother and I go way back. His father died a few years back, and Nelson had to drop out of college."

"Then someone told me how I could make money dancing," Nelson said, "so now I can afford to get my education. I plan to transfer to Duke once I get my associate's degree here."

Lillian nodded. "He does most of his work in Athens, but he agreed to perform for us tonight." She looked at Nelson. "Now Darla's probably going to ask you to take everything off, but I'm warning you right now, I'll call your mama if you do."

"Don't worry," he said, grinning. "I do have some modesty left in me."

Lillian looked at Annie. "You need to go call Darla."

"Do you have everything you need?" Annie asked the man.

"Yeah, got it all right here. How strong is your coffee table?"

Annie's look went blank. "I beg your pardon?"

"It's strong enough," Lillian said, rushing over to clear the food trays and set them on the dining table instead. "I've seen your routine. If you break the coffee table, I'll just buy another one."

Annie hurried toward the bedroom and placed her call to Darla. "Please come quick," she told her friend. "It's my ankle. I think I may have broken it this time. I need you to drive me to the emergency room."

Darla was clearly upset. "Annie Hartford, I told you and told you to stay off that ankle. I don't know how you think you're going to work the Okra Festival with a broken ankle. And how I'm supposed to get you down that flight of stairs by myself? Should I go look for Bo?"

"No, don't bother him. I can get down the stairs by myself. I do it all the time. Just hurry."

"Hang in there, kiddo. It won't take me more than ten minutes."

Annie made her way back to the living room, where she discovered everyone except Nelson held a plastic cup of wine. "Okay, the bride-to-be is on her way," she said.

"Good." Lillian shoved a cup of wine at her. "Let's party."

Darla arrived in gray sweats and curlers. She burst through the front door and froze in horror when everyone shouted surprise. Nelson gave her a kiss on the cheek and led her to a chair in front of the coffee table as Kazue handed her a glass of wine.

"It's your bachelorette party," Inge said.

Darla tossed Annie a dark look as she plucked the pink spongy curlers from her hair, leaving fat sausage-roll curls in their place. "I'm gonna get you for this, Hartford. The least you could've done was give me time to make myself presentable."

"Honey, you're beautiful," Nelson said, going to his boom box.

"I like this guy," Darla replied.

The music started, "Honky-Tonk Woman" by the Rolling Stones. Nelson danced around the apartment, stopping to rub up against the guests while Lillian filled their glasses with more wine. Annie chuckled when he came up to her and kissed her lightly on the cheek. Finally, he turned to Darla as a bump-and-grind routine began, and he danced just for her. Nelson stepped up on the coffee table in his bare feet and began to move in a way that had all the women squealing. He reached for his bow tie, pulled it free, and tossed it to Darla.

"Take it off, baby," Lillian shouted, sending the women into a fit of giggles.

His jacket and vest came off in one tug, and he was soon bare from the waist up. He motioned for Darla, who stood eagerly, and he pulled her onto the coffee table with him. Annie decided it was the first time she'd ever seen her friend blush. Luckily, Cheryl had brought a camera and took pictures of the whole thing.

The music slowed and Darla jumped down. Nelson spent the next few minutes flexing his muscles and making suggestive movements that worked the women into a frenzy. Lillian came through with more wine, and the pace of the music quickened. Nelson took off his cummerbund and tossed it at Lillian, then one quick jerk and his pants disappeared, leaving him in a thong bikini. The women went wild. Inge fanned herself with a magazine. He motioned for Annie to step forward, and all the women in the room yelled their encouragement.

Outside, Sam could hear the screaming over the loud music and decided it was time to investigate. It sounded as if Annie was in a lot of trouble.

He shot up the stairs and through the front door like a bullet, then stood there dumbly as he watched a barefoot Annie dance far too close to an almost naked man. Everybody was so wrapped up in the show they didn't notice him. This was not the Annie he'd come to care about, he told himself as he watched the two dance in a way that would have gotten them kicked out of most places. He shook his head sadly.

Just as he started for the door Annie saw him. She looked surprised and a lot embarrassed. "Sam, what on earth are you doing here?" she asked. She climbed off the coffee table and Kazue took her place. Annie hurried over to Sam, noting the dark scowl on his face. "What's wrong?" she asked.

Sam was glad the other women were so involved with the show that they paid him no mind. "What's wrong?" he repeated. "I thought you were studying, Annie. Imagine my surprise to walk in here and find you dancing with a naked man." He gave a snort. "That's not even dancing. Looks more like you're mating with him in front of the whole neighborhood. This is a helluva party you're giving, Annie. Once word gets out, you just might end up being the most popular girl in town."

Annie felt her temper flare. "That's not a very nice thing to say to me," she said testily. "Had you bothered to call first—"

"Oh, I get it. I'm not allowed to drop by, because God only knows what you'll be doing. Well, you just go ahead and party. I certainly don't want to interfere with your fun."

Annie could see that he was hurt as well as angry, but that didn't give him the right to barge in uninvited and falsely accuse her. "You don't know what you're talking about, Sam Ballard. Please leave before you ruin everybody's fun."

"Oh, gladly." He turned and stalked down the stairs. Sam drove straight to his office, where he tried to cool off and catch up on paperwork. But he couldn't get the image of Annie dancing with that man out of his mind. And she must've liked it because she'd had a smile on her face a mile wide. He didn't appreciate any man dancing with his woman.

His woman. Oh, for Pete's sake!

Just because he wanted her to be his didn't make it so. He thought of dancing with her as the young man had, and he instantly grew hard. He only had to take one look at her, and his testosterone level shot straight through the ceiling. Maybe it was his ego talking, but he suspected she wanted him just a little bit too.

Well, hell. There was only one way to find out.

Sam checked his wristwatch. It was after nine, surely Annie's company had gone home by now. If they hadn't, he'd wait on her front steps till they did. Let the women think what they wished, he didn't care. He was going to find out how Annie felt about him no matter what. Even if it was bad news, he needed to know.

He made the drive in less than five minutes and parked in the driveway in front of the garage. He took the steps two at a time, then paused at the front door and listened. There was no music, no laughter, nothing. Annie was alone.

He knocked. Annie opened the door a moment later wearing a nightgown and bathrobe. He walked in and closed the door behind him. She didn't look happy to see him, but he didn't care. He was going to have his say and get out.

"I don't know what you're all about, Annie Hartford, but if you're a party girl, then I'll try to accommodate you."

She crossed her arms. "Sam, what the hell are you talking about?"

"You seemed to enjoy having that young stud's hands all over you."

She sighed wearily. "Is that what you think, Sam?" she demanded, her anger flaring.

He hesitated for the first time. "That's the way it looked."

"Well, let me tell you one thing, Sam Ballard. First of all, you had no right to walk into my house without knocking—"

"I heard screaming."

"Second, you will not stand in judgment of how I live my life. Not you or anybody else. Is that clear?"

"Yes," he said tightly.

She smiled. "I'm glad we've settled that. Now, if you really want to feel like an idiot, here it is. The truth is, you walked in on Darla's bachelorette party, and you saw a bunch of women letting their hair down. Everybody danced with that guy, and we had a ball doing it."

Sam stared at her. "That was Darla's bachelorette party? Why didn't you tell me you were throwing one for her? I never would have come around had I known that. Is that why you were in such a hurry to leave the picnic?"

"Yes. And I didn't tell you because I'd been sworn to secrecy. Besides, I'm not obligated to tell you every move I make."

Sam really did feel like a fool. He began pacing. "Gee, I don't know what to say, Annie. I'm sorry. I'm sorry for acting like a fool, for being so insanely jealous, I couldn't think straight. But most of all I'm sorry for thinking the worst of you." He raked both hands through his hair. "My only excuse is that I'm crazy about you. And I want you. I want you so bad it hurts.

"I'm a jerk, that's what I am. I have no business coming around here, spying on you, interfering with your life. All I can say is I'm sorry, and that I'll stay away from now on." He knew it was going to be a hard promise to keep, but after all he'd done, he had no choice. He reached for the doorknob.

"Sam, wait!" Annie stepped closer. His apology had touched her deeply; his confession had left her wanting him as badly as he claimed to want her. "Don't go."

Sam realized he was breathing heavily. "Annie, I shouldn't stay."

She placed her hand tenderly on his chest. His heart thumped wildly. "Please stay."

His eyes searched her face as though he were trying to reach inside her and find out what was going on. He finally closed them and sighed heavily. He could not be in the same room with her without wanting to touch her. And touching her was dangerous. His control had snapped a long time ago. "Babe, you don't know what you're asking."

Her own eyes were filled with promises and a deep longing. "I'm a big girl. I know exactly what I'm asking." She felt his nipple harden beneath her fingers. She drew a circle around it. Sam grasped her wrist, and their gazes locked.

"Dammit, Annie, I wanted you from the first moment I laid eyes on you," he said. "I saw you in that bridal gown, and it angered me that you were meant for someone else." He shook his head. "And when I saw you in Darla's uniform, it was like someone had kicked me in the stomach. I couldn't take my eyes off you."

"So I noticed. Why do you think I kept breaking plates?" Annie began unbuttoning his shirt.

"And it made me mad as hell." He glanced down. "What are you doing?"

She pulled his shirttail from his slacks. His chest was broad and hair-roughened. "Well, now, Mr. Ballard. You make Nelson look like a young boy."

Sam studied her face, thought he saw desire there, prayed he wasn't wrong. "Annie, are you trying to seduce me?"

She smiled and lifted her face to his. "Yes. How do you think I'm doing so far?"

"You're doing great. Please don't let me stop you." He kissed her again, this time slowly, leisurely, as though he had all the time in the world. Once his tongue had explored the depths of her mouth, he cupped her face between his palms and kissed her closed eyelids, her forehead, then her chin. He cupped her breasts and groaned aloud.

"Sam Ballard?"

"Hmm?"

"I think you are about the best-looking thing I've seen in a long time. And I would gladly have told you in the beginning had you not been wearing a smirk."

He felt her nipples tighten. "I had to smirk to disguise how much I wanted to run after you. Every time I caught sight of you in that short skirt, my blood pressure shot up."

"So, you like me?"

He chuckled. "Like really doesn't come close to what I feel for you. I've been through pure hell today worrying about you, wondering if you were seeing someone else. Made a damn fool of myself."

"I thought it was sweet." She nuzzled his chest hair. "And guess what? I'd much rather dance with you." She nipped one nipple with her teeth, and he drew a long shaky breath. "Want to follow me to my lair?" Annie asked.

Sam chuckled. "I love it when you talk dirty." Without warning, he swept her high in his arms and carried her into the bedroom. He laid her gently on the bed, showering kisses along her jaw and down her throat. Annie shivered.

He pulled off her gown, and the sight of her breasts took his breath away. This time she wore flesh-colored bikini underwear. He kneaded her breasts gently with his hands, then closed his mouth around one rosy nipple. He teased the other, rolling it between his thumb and forefinger until it quivered.

Annie sighed her immense pleasure as every part of her body responded to Sam's caresses. His lips moved from her breasts, skimming her stomach and pausing only briefly at her navel while he pulled off her panties. He could not resist exploring the tuft of hair between her thighs. He smiled when he found her wet.

Sam wasted no time undressing. Annie had climbed beneath the sheets, and he took great pleasure in peeling the covers off of her. He kissed her on the lips once more before tracing a path with his tongue to her femininity. He inhaled her essence, enjoying a brief moment of dizziness before tasting her for the first time.

Annie cried out and arched her body as Sam's tongue boldly explored the honeyed area between her thighs. He found the sensitive nub and tongued it until she could no longer hold back. Her orgasm took her breath away and made him desire her all the more.

When at last he entered her, Sam thought he had surely died and gone to heaven. She gripped him so tightly, it was all he could do to keep from exploding. He heard her ragged breathing and realized she had become aroused once more. He began to move faster, pressing deep inside. Annie cried out once more, and a second later he emptied himself inside of her.

Afterward, Annie lay in his arms, smiling contentedly as Sam stroked her. They dozed, and when Annie opened her eyes again, Sam was hard and ready for her. "Oh, my," she said. "I think we may have started something."

ELEVEN

When Annie opened her eyes the second time, Sam was propped on one elbow, watching her. "I'm starved," he said. "Is there anything to eat around here?"

"You're in luck," she said. "There are leftovers from the party in my refrigerator. Wanna raid it?"

Ten minutes later they were sitting at the dining-room table eating finger sandwiches and chips and dip. "Man, do I love Sunday," Sam said. "It's the only day of the week I can really relax."

"What about your convenience stores? Don't you have to check on them?"

He shook his head. "The night managers do everything. The money goes straight into a safe. My stores aren't open all night. We close at ten for safety purposes. Not that Pinckney is what you'd refer to as a dangerous town," he added. "And I don't have to do anything for the car wash except go by and get the change out. If something breaks down, I call someone in to fix it, and that's about it."

"I would imagine the restaurant takes up most of your time," Annie said.

He nodded. "I've been thinking of making Darla manager." He held up a finger. "That's just between you and me."

Annie made a production of zipping her lip. "I think Darla would make a wonderful manager."

"And it would free me up," he said. "I've got too many things going on. I'd sell the whole lot if I could get a good price. Use the money to buy cattle. Go back to farming."

"What about that law degree you worked so hard to get?"

He shrugged. "I could practice out of my home. My office there is big enough."

Annie propped herself on one elbow as well. "So what else are you going to do with all that spare time?"

Sam lost his train of thought when she licked some of the dip from her bottom lip. "I might like to court a certain lady if she's interested. 'Course, she's going to have to give up all her young studs and settle for a broken down thirty-five-year-old."

Annie tossed him a saucy smile. "I have a feeling this young lady is partial to senior citizens."

"Well, now, I do believe I've been challenged to prove myself capable in the bedroom once again."

She chuckled. "No, Sam, you have already proven yourself capable several times over. Right now I need sleep."

He stroked her cheek. "Okay, babe." They finished their snack and began cleaning up. "When do you think your father is going to start looking for you?" he asked.

She shrugged. "He may decide not to."

"No way, Annie. You're heir to a multimillion-dollar estate, and you've got his limo. He's going to look."

"He can look for me all he wants," she said, "but I'm not going back to live with him. I like my life just the way it is."

"Begging your pardon, but I can't see you staying on as a waitress for very long. It's hard work."

"I'm not afraid of hard work."

"I realize that, but I don't think you're going to get much personal satisfaction out of it."

"Why do you think I'm taking courses?" she said, pointing to her books. "One day I'm going to hang my shingle out front. Anne Hartford, CPA."

Sam smiled. "That would make you proud, wouldn't it?"

"Darn right."

"Most women in your position would be more than happy to live off their inheritance."

"I'm not most women."

"So I've noticed." He gazed at her lazily. If he'd thought her beautiful when he'd first seen her, nothing compared with the woman before him now. In her short nightgown with her hair mussed and her skin still flushed from lovemaking, she was a vision.

"Stop looking at me that way, Sam. It's after midnight."

He looked surprised. "What way, Annie?"

"As if you know what I look like beneath my nightgown."

"I *do* know what you look like underneath it, and it's making me crazy. But I'm going to leave and let you get your beauty rest. Not that you could look more beautiful than you do tonight." He kissed her deeply. "Do you need a ride to school tomorrow morning, or is your dance partner going to pick you up on his tricycle?"

She laughed and threw her arms around his neck. "You are so bad."

"Damn right I am. And don't ever forget it." But he was smiling and didn't look quite as threatening as he sounded.

Annie raised her lips to his for one last kiss. When Sam pulled away, he sighed. "Damn, I'd stay with you all night, if I weren't worried about your reputation. Be thankful you've got a gentleman on your hands."

Annie remembered the way they'd spent the past few hours. "You, sir, are no gentleman, and I, for one, am very glad of that fact." She offered him a beguiling smile. "Good night, Sam," she said softly, once he released her. A minute later he was on the stairs, heading for his car. Annie felt a sudden emptiness that frightened her. As she locked up, it hit her: She had gone and fallen in love with Sam Ballard.

Annie rode her bicycle to school Monday morning and shared a secret smile with Nelson. "You do a mean bump-and-grind routine, kiddo," she said as they walked from their first class to the next one. "Thank you for making the party such a big success."

"Hey, I'll dance for you anytime, pretty lady. Perhaps you'd like a private showing. Say this weekend, after I take you to dinner?"

Annie laughed. "Get real, Nelson, I'm old enough to be—" She paused and thought. "Your older sister."

"You're not that much older than me. Think about it and give me a call." He handed her a business card that read DANCER EXTRAORDINAIRE. Beside it was a man in the tux, and a telephone number below.

"Actually, Nelson," she began in a whisper, "I think I've fallen in love."

"No kidding?" He leaned close. "Then he's a very lucky man, Annie."

Once class ended, Annie rode her bike to the Dixieland Café, grabbed her books and paper sack, and changed into her uniform. She noted the activity going on in the courthouse square and questioned Darla about the upcoming Okra Festival.

"It's just something we do every year to get folks to visit," she said. "There'll be a parade to sort of kick things off, and a bunch of crafters and food vendors. It's kinda fun, but we're so busy, we don't have time to enjoy much. Except for on Sunday," she added with a smile.

Annie made a mental note to ride her bike to the secondhand store the following morning since she didn't have class on Tuesdays. She hoped she could find something presentable. Sam came in wearing a scowl, and Darla laughed.

"He gets this way every year," she said to Annie, " 'cause he has to wear his okra suit. Hey, Sam, did you remember to get Mr. Okra out of the dry cleaners?" Darla asked, loud enough for the whole restaurant to hear.

"Very funny, Darla," he muttered.

"Okra suit?" Annie asked. Both corners of her mouth twitched. "What in heaven's name is that?"

"It's something the town officials came up with to humiliate business owners," he said with a growl. "And it works."

"He looks pretty damn stupid in it too," Flo shouted through the food-order window.

Annie chuckled. "I do believe I am looking forward to this event," she drawled in a syrupy voice.

"Don't push it, Annie," he said, although there was a distinct softening in his tone. He glanced around the restaurant. "Nobody makes any wisecracks while I'm in costume, or they're fired."

"Oh, gee," Darla said. "I'm going to start making my list right away."

"I got a word for you right now," Patricia said, peeking through the swinging door. "Dumb. Why they want folks to dress up like okra is beyond my comprehension."

"Because the citizens of Pinckney want people to stand back and take a good look at their fine little town," Sam replied. "And I'm willing to look goofy one day a year in order to accomplish that."

"And it has nothing to do with the fact that your businesses take in enough money to sink a barge," Darla said, her voice tinged with sarcasm.

Sam regarded her. "Do I look like a man who'd wear a stupid okra outfit for nothing, Darla Mae?"

The customers started coming in, and everybody got busy. The lunchtime crowd was heavier than usual, as was the dinner crowd. "Some folks come early," Darla said. "Tomorrow this place'll be jammin'. By the way, have you found a dress yet?"

"Plan to get it tomorrow," Annie said.

The restaurant cleared out by nine-thirty. Flo and Patricia were already gone, and Darla waved a weary good-bye as she hurried home to Bo. "Want me to give you a ride home?" Sam asked Annie. "I can put your bike in the back of my Jeep."

"I was hoping you'd ask," she told him.

After arriving at her apartment, Annie invited Sam in. He put her bike in the garage and joined her upstairs. He pulled her into his arms the minute he stepped inside. "Promise me one thing," he said, after a series of hungry kisses.

"Anything," she said.

"Promise you'll still respect me after you see me dressed like a vegetable."

She chuckled. "I'm all grungy. I think I'll take a quick shower. Want to join me?" She started down the hall, and Sam followed, wearing a huge grin.

When Annie woke up the following morning, Sam was gone, but he'd left a note on her pillow, a simple thank-you inside a heart. She smiled as she remembered how they'd spent a portion of the night. She was falling hard, she thought. She drank two cups of coffee as she straightened the apartment and dressed for her shopping trip, pulling a jacket over her sweater to fight the chill.

"I've been holding a couple of dresses for you," the lady at the secondhand store said the minute Annie walked through the door. "Lillian Calhoun told me you needed one for Darla's wedding." She brought out two creations that had matching shoes.

Annie chose a simple, mint-green crepe dress with a matching bolero jacket that added a touch of sophistication. "The shoes are a little loose," she said.

"Stuff cotton balls into the toes," the woman told her. "Works every time."

When Annie arrived back at her apartment, Lillian came running out her back door with a basket of fresh-cut flowers. "I told the florist she could leave them with me," she said. "Wonder who they're from?"

"Gee, I haven't a clue," Annie replied innocently.

"Bet they're from the person whose Jeep sat in the driveway till late last night." When Annie blushed, Lillian laughed. "Don't worry, your secret is safe with me. But all folks have to do is see the two of you together, and they'll know."

"You think so?" Annie said.

"Honey, you both shine like new pennies when you're in each other's company."

"But it happened so fast."

"Then it was meant to be." She noted the brown bag. "Oh, you've been to the secondhand store. I would have driven you. Let me see what you got."

Lillian made a fuss over Annie's selection. "Tell you what. I'll run it by the dry cleaners this morning and it'll be out in time for the wedding. You don't need to worry about that on top of work and school." She nudged her and winked. "And romance."

"You're too kind," Annie told her.

"Hey, that's just the way it is here," the woman replied.

As Annie prepared for work she realized that *was* the way things were in Pinckney. She had never known such kindness and concern. And such happiness. Especially since one Sam Ballard had stepped into her life.

On Friday, when Annie arrived at work, the restaurant was packed. The morning-shift waitress was still there, and Darla was helping her. "It's going to be a long day," she said to Annie as she passed by with a tray of water glasses.

The lunch shift was much busier than usual, and it was all Annie could do to keep up. Fortunately, Sam had hired a man to bus tables and wash dishes, so it wasn't as bad as it could have been. Sam walked in shortly before one in his okra outfit, and Annie had to look away quickly in order to keep from bursting into laughter.

"Is everything okay?" he asked her as she was getting iced tea for a table of eight.

"Yes, fine." Her tone was serious, her words clipped.

"What's wrong?"

"Nothing."

"Something's wrong," he said. "I can read you like a book."

A giggle escaped her. "Sam, please don't bother me right now."

"It's this outfit, right? Am I right?" he said when she didn't answer. "Is that why you won't look at me?"

Laughter bubbled up from her throat. "Go away, Sam," she ordered. "I can't work with you here."

"It's not *that* funny."

"Yes, it is. Trust me."

"I have to go," he said, sounding a little hurt. "The parade starts in ten minutes. I'll be back to help out as soon as I can."

"By the way, thanks for the flowers. They're beautiful."

"You really like them?"

She chanced a look in his direction and swallowed a giggle. "Yes. But not half as much as I like you."

"I wish I could kiss you right here," he said.

"Me too. But don't. There's a truck driver in the second booth who just proposed marriage. If he thinks I'm hot for Okra Man, he might lose interest."

"You tell that slick-talking trucker you belong to someone else," Sam said. "And if you're not here when I get back, I'm going to comb every truck stop between Miami and Portland. Nobody runs off with my woman."

His woman. Annie liked the sound of it.

Most of the people cleared out in time for the parade, and those who came in took seats next to the window. There was the sound of a siren, and the next thing Annie knew, a marching band was standing right in front of the restaurant playing a lively tune. She and Darla stood at the counter sharing a club sandwich and fries, and Flo and Patricia watched from the door, Patricia stepping out from time to time to snap a picture with her camera. They all fell into a fit of laughter when Sam and a dozen other men marched through in okra outfits. Flo laughed so hard, she had to sit in a booth to recover.

Once the restaurant completely cleared, Darla and Annie filled the sugar canisters, wiped condiments, and got the place ready for the dinner crowd. Annie made up salads and stuck them into an oversized refrigerator while Darla cleaned the long counter, the stools, and all the other seats. Flo and Patricia readied the kitchen while the dishwasher finished the last of the pots and pans. When everything was straight, they all took a well-deserved break.

The place literally sparkled when Sam walked through the door. "Did we have a good lunch crowd?" he asked Darla as he poured himself a cup of coffee.

"We had an awesome crowd. And Annie kept up just fine. You shoulda seen her coming through that door with those big food trays piled high. Looked like a pro."

Annie mouthed a silent thank-you to her friend for not mentioning the two plates and the coffee cup she had broken. "It was nice having someone clean our tables," she said. "And I'm sure the girls in back appreciated having someone to wash dishes."

Sam nodded. "I might keep him on for a while. You girls shouldn't have to work as hard as you do."

"My, my, you are awfully sweet to think of us, Sammy," Darla said. "I just can't help but wonder about this sudden change of heart, especially since I've been begging for a busboy for years."

"You know what they say about looking a gift horse in the mouth," Darla Mae." Sam drained his coffee and stood. "I'm going to my office and change out of this ridiculous thing and check my phone messages. Call me if you need me." He looked at Annie and smiled before walking out the door.

"Well, now, ain't that something," Darla said, once Sam had left. "I never thought I'd live to see the day. Sam Ballard in love."

"Really?" Annie said weakly.

"Oh, honey, it's written all over his face. He tries to act so cool when there are other people around, I reckon he's not ready to share his feelings with the rest of us—but that man is smitten. Cupid has done shot his arrow right through Sam's heart." She gazed intently at Annie. "So what are you going to do about it?"

Annie was at a loss. "I've no idea."

TWELVE

For four days Annie and Darla raced about the Dixieland Café, trying to keep up with the lunch and dinner
crowds. Sam had pulled in another girl to help with the
breakfast shift as well. Between classes, studying, and
trying to keep the pace at work, Annie lost four pounds.

Darla was terrified of losing weight. "I paid that alterations lady a small fortune to take up that gown, I sure
don't want to have to go back to her."

Annie was thankful when Sunday finally arrived, and
the restaurant closed. She got up early and rode her
bicycle to the festival and visited the booths. She purchased inexpensive gifts for all her new friends, and ordered a double helping of fried okra from one of the
vendors. She was surprised to realize how many people
she knew, many of them regular patrons of the Dixieland. They were all eager to know how she liked living
in Pinckney, how her classes were going, and if she was
comfortable living in Lillian's garage apartment. It
amazed her that in just a short time she'd come to feel at

home in the small town. She ran into Bic Fenwick, the mechanic, and apologized for not doing something about the limo.

"Hey, no problem, Miss Hartford. Folks get a real kick out of it. Actually, I think it brings in more business, and I have plenty of room for it out back. You just take your time, okay?"

Annie checked her watch and saw that it was getting late. She had three hours before she was to be back for Darla's wedding. She rode her bike home and put it in the garage. Lillian called her from the back door of her house. She was holding a plastic bag containing Annie's dress.

"I knocked on your door this morning, but you weren't home. I thought you might need this."

"Thank you, Lillian. What do I owe you?"

"Forget it, hon. It wasn't that much."

"Here, I have something for you," Annie said. "I picked it up at the festival this morning." She pulled out a pack of notecards and envelopes adorned with magnolias.

"Oh, how lovely!" Lillian exclaimed. "But I don't want you spending your hard-earned money on me. You need to be saving it."

"It's not much," Annie said. "Just something to show my appreciation for all you've done."

Lillian kissed her on the cheek. "Well, you're a real sweetheart, and I thank you. By the way, do you need a ride to Darla's wedding, or is that handsome Sam Ballard picking you up?"

"He's picking me up. I've offered to help him at the reception." She glanced at her wristwatch. "I'd better get cleaned up. Thanks again for taking care of my dress."

"I'll see you at the ceremony," Lillian said, hurrying toward her house as well.

Annie straightened her place, took a hot shower, and spent a long time on her makeup. Once her hair dried, she sprayed it and finger-combed the waves and curls so that it came out fuller. She did her nails and waited till they were dry to begin dressing. She stuffed cotton balls in the toes of the shoes until they felt snug. Checking her reflection in the mirror, she was pleased with what she saw. She put on lipstick, sprayed herself with an inexpensive perfume she'd picked up, and pronounced herself ready.

Sam arrived ten minutes later looking dapper in a charcoal suit, crisp white dress shirt, and burgundy tie. He whistled when he caught sight of Annie. "Don't you know it's not good to outshine the bride," he said.

"The bride will be wearing a ten-thousand-dollar gown. She's spent half the day having her hair and nails done, I seriously doubt she's going to get any competition from me."

He pulled her into his arms. "Trust me, Annie. You'll be the most beautiful woman there. And if you didn't have all that lipstick on you, I'd kiss you senseless right here and now."

"Oh, my, we can't get into that now, can we? We might end up missing the wedding."

"Hey, do me a favor," Sam said, "Pack a bag." When she arched one blond eyebrow, he grinned. "Martha left town for a couple of days to see her sister." He captured her hands. "I would very much like it if you'd spend the night at my place. You might as well bring your books as well. That way I can drive you straight to school in the morning."

"Spend the night at your place?" she asked. "I hadn't considered that."

"Please say yes, Annie. The reception is only going to last a couple of hours. We'll have the whole place to ourselves."

She squeezed his hands. "Of course I'm going to say yes. Why wouldn't I want to spend every moment I can with you?"

He looked pleased. "Good answer, Annie."

"Let me get my things, okay?" She hurried down the hall to her bedroom and packed a paper sack with all she'd need, including her waitress uniform, which she'd already washed. She grabbed her books and carried everything to the living room.

Sam took the books from her. "We're going to have to buy you a nice overnight bag," he said. "I can't have my girlfriend lugging her belongings in a paper sack." He grinned and opened the door, then swatted her behind as she went out.

Annie tossed him a cool look. "You are certainly taking a lot of liberties with me these days, Mr. Ballard."

He laughed. "Honey, you ain't seen nothing yet."

The bride and groom had not yet arrived when Sam and Annie took their places on the bandstand. The band itself had been moved to a grassy area nearby so the wedding would take place on the raised platform where everyone could see. People stood or sat in lawn chairs, patiently awaiting the couple. They began clapping when a white carriage and two white horses made its way down the cobblestone street that surrounded the courthouse. The band began playing the "Wedding March." There was a lot of oohing and ahhing as the groom descended and reached for his bride's hand. Annie felt a huge lump in her throat as the sight of Darla in the gown. She look at Sam and found him watching her. He winked once.

Sam nudged Annie. "Here, I almost forgot. Darla gave these to me yesterday." He held two simple gold wedding bands. Annie picked up the larger of the two, knowing she would be expected to hand it to Darla, who would then slip it on Bo's finger while saying her vows. She slipped it on her thumb and held Darla's train as the woman made her way up the stairs. Then she moved to the left of her friend as Sam took his place to the right of Bo.

When the music died down, the minister stepped forward, and a hush fell over the crowd. The only sound Annie heard was the clicking of cameras. Darla's wedding would probably end up on the front page of the *Pinckney Gazette*.

The minister stepped forward. "Dearly beloved . . ." he began.

Annie was only vaguely aware of what he said as she and Sam kept exchanging looks. She wondered what he was thinking, wondered if he knew how devastatingly handsome he looked. Most of all, she wondered if he suspected she'd fallen in love with him.

". . . The ring please."

Annie handed Darla the ring, and she felt her eyes

mist as her friend vowed to love the man beside her forever. She knew the couple had been through a lot of heartache, and she hoped the future would bring them nothing but happiness. Next, it was Sam's turn to hand over a ring, and she listened as Bo repeated the words Darla had said a moment before. The minister pronounced them husband and wife, and the two kissed as shouts and whistles rang out from the crowd below.

Darla hugged Annie, both of them crying. "Thank you for the dress, honey. And thank you for helping to make this the best day of my life." Bo and Sam shook hands, and Sam kissed Darla, slipping her an envelope. "This is for your honeymoon. I know Bo just started a new job, but hang on to this, maybe in a few months he can get some time off."

"Oh, Sam, you're the best," Darla said, hugging him hard.

Sam's eyes were soft as his gaze landed on Annie. He offered her his arm. "May I be your escort to the reception, Miss Hartford?" he asked. She smiled and took his arm.

They were the first to arrive at Sam's house. A catering service was on standby, and they went to work, filling buckets with ice for the champagne, bringing out trays of food. There was a small table holding a wedding cake, and numerous white and gold balloons hovered overhead. "It's beautiful," Annie said.

"I was up all night baking this cake and making hors d'oeuvres and blowing up balloons," Sam told her. Nearby, the lady who owned the catering service chuckled. "Don't give me away," Sam said. "I'm trying to impress the lady."

Annie laughed. "I'm already impressed, honey," she said, patting his hand. "I'm here with you, aren't I?"

"You probably just came 'cause you heard there was going to be good food and champagne."

They kept up the lively banter until the guests arrived. Someone had helped Darla remove her train, and as she squeezed through the front door in the gown, Annie thought she looked radiant. The two women hugged as Sam listed the qualities of a good husband, the most important being to take the trash out every night.

"What do you know about marriage, Sam Ballard?" Lillian said, coming through the door. "You've been single all your life. Don't you think it's about time you found a good woman and tied the knot?"

Sam's gaze automatically landed on Annie, who in turn blushed and had the crowd laughing.

"That might not be such a bad idea, Lillian," he said. "But first I have to find somebody who'll have me."

Annie was relieved when the caterer opened the bottles of champagne and it was time to make a toast. Although Sam had made it sound as though he'd invited only a handful of people, she suspected there were between thirty and forty guests.

Once everyone had eaten their fill, Bo and Darla bid their farewells and hurried to her car while the guests threw birdseed. Annie knew they were going back to their mobile home, and she wondered if Darla would be able to get through the door in her gown or if she'd have to take it off the way she, Annie, had. When she looked up at Sam, he was smiling, and she wondered if he was thinking the same thing.

The guests left, and the caterers, who'd been cleaning

up all along, took only a few minutes to get their things together. Sam, who was sitting on the sofa, grabbed Annie around the waist and pulled her onto his lap. He kissed her hard. "I thought they'd never leave."

She smiled. "It was a wonderful reception. The food was excellent and everybody had a great time."

"I wouldn't know, Miss Hartford. My eyes were on you. You seem to have made a lot of friends here in very little time. In fact, I think my woman is quite popular with the townspeople."

She arched one eyebrow. "Your woman?"

"That's right. You got a problem with that?"

She leaned against him. He'd loosened his tie and dispensed with his jacket. She could feel the heat of his body through his dress shirt. "Does that mean you're my man?"

"Baby, I was yours the moment I first laid eyes on you."

Annie closed her eyes, basking in the moment. She had never felt so close to him. He turned her face to his and kissed her deeply. Still holding her in his arms, he stood and carried her to his bedroom.

Their lovemaking was slow and tender. Sam explored every inch of Annie's body. When she reached out to him, he entered her, and their sighs of pleasure wafted upward. Annie climaxed, and Sam followed right behind her.

Later they held on to each other as they waited for their breathing to return to normal. Finally, Sam looked into her eyes. "I love you, Annie Hartford."

Her insides fluttered. "I love you, too, Sam."

❖━━━━━❖

Life got back to normal the following week, although Darla drove everyone crazy with honeymoon brochures. By Friday, she had narrowed it down to either a cabin in the mountains in Gatlinburg, Tennessee, or a week in Key West, Florida. Bo was doing all he could to hold her off until the first of the year so he could get some time under his belt at his new job.

Annie and Darla were cleaning up after the lunch crowd when a dove-gray Mercedes Benz parked out front. Annie took one look at it, and her heart sank clear to her toes.

"Would'ja get a load of that," Darla said. "Wonder who it is?"

"I know who it is," Annie said dully as a tall blond-haired man in expensive clothes and two-hundred-dollar sunglasses climbed out. He made his way to the front door, opened it, and stared at Annie for a full minute before saying anything. "Hello, Annie. You're looking good." He took his sunglasses off. "That uniform becomes you."

"Hello, Eldon." Her tone was lifeless. "What are you doing here?"

"Is there somewhere we can be alone?" His gaze went to Darla, who was pretending not to listen as she wiped down the long counter.

"This is a close friend of mine," Annie replied. "Whatever you have to say to me, you can say in front of her."

"I have bad news, Annie. Your father suffered a heart

attack a week ago. He's dying. I thought you might want to see him—" He paused. "Before it's too late."

Annie was only vaguely aware when Sam opened the door and stepped in. The smile on his face faltered when he saw the expression on Annie's. "What's wrong?" he asked.

Annie realized she was trembling "I have to go back to Atlanta, Sam."

"What!"

She untied her apron and laid it on the counter. "It's my father." She looked at Darla. "I'm sorry to leave you like this."

"Hey, no problem, kiddo. You do whatcha gotta do."

"And tell Lillian? I'm not sure how long I'll be gone."

Sam took in the guy standing near the door. "Who are you?"

"Eldon Wentworth; who are you?"

Sam stepped closer. "I'm the man who's going to marry Annie, that's who."

If the news had an impact on Eldon one way or another, he didn't show it. "You might have to put the nuptials on hold for a while, my friend. Annie's got more pressing business to attend to."

Annie started for the door, but Sam stopped her. "Annie, don't go."

She could see the pain in his eyes. "I have to, Sam. My father's dying."

"Then let me drive you." His voice pleaded with her.

"I don't know how long—" She paused to get a grip on her emotions. "Please don't make this harder than it is. I'm in a hurry to get going."

Sam saw the devastation in her eyes and backed off. "You know my number, Annie. Call me. I have to know that you're okay."

She nodded and followed Eldon out to his car. She didn't allow the tears to fall until he'd pulled away. "When did he have the heart attack?" she asked, once they were on their way.

"The day after the wedding," he replied gently.

She twisted her hands in her lap. "It's all my fault, then."

Eldon covered her hands with his. "Don't blame yourself, Annie. It won't get you anywhere. I've been trying to find you since it happened."

"How *did* you find me?"

"Through your Social Security number." He drove in silence for a while. Annie cried quietly. "I want you to know I don't hold any grudges for what happened," Eldon said.

"I'm sorry if I embarrassed you," Annie told him. "I felt pressured into marrying you from the beginning."

"You know how your father feels about you. He wants to make sure you're taken care of when he's gone. I just don't think he intended to go this fast."

She sniffed. "I don't need someone to take care of me. I was doing fine on my own."

"Oh, come on, Annie. Working as a waitress?"

"I'm not going to make excuses for earning an honest living. I was also going to school."

"Good for you. I know how important a good education is to you. What were you studying?"

Annie wondered if he was really interested or just

making conversation. "Accounting. I plan to get my degree in it so I can find a good job, then I'm going to work toward my master's."

Eldon patted her hand. "I always knew you had it in you, hon. You're smart as a whip."

"Funny, you never mentioned it before now," she said dully.

"I knew your father had old-fashioned beliefs about women, and I didn't feel it was my place to argue with him. I'd sort of hoped you go back to school after we got married."

"Oh? And what about the passel of grandchildren your mother wanted."

He gave her a half smile. "Honey, we're adults. We'd make our own decisions. Not your father and certainly not my mother." He sighed. "I wish you'd come to me with your concerns. Perhaps we could have prevented this misunderstanding."

"It's not important now," she said.

"That guy back there. He sounded pretty serious about you. Are you in love with him?"

"No more questions, Eldon," she said. Annie leaned back and closed her eyes.

They arrived at the hospital several hours later. Eldon tried to explain the situation as they hurried to the elevators. "He's in the cardiac-care unit, Annie. They'll only let you in for a few minutes."

"That's enough." It would give her time to apologize for what she'd done. They stepped off the elevator and followed the signs to CCU. When they entered the waiting area, Annie saw several of her father's closest friends. The looks on their faces stopped her cold. "How is he?" she asked in a shaky voice.

Carl Yeager, her father's lawyer and trusted friend, took Annie in his arms. "Your father passed away twenty minutes ago, dear. I'm so terribly sorry."

THIRTEEN

The guilt was the worst part, Annie discovered. As usual, her father had planned his funeral to the last detail, so it and the burial went off without a hitch. Annie was surprised to see Sam, Darla, and Lillian in the crowd of mourners. She acknowledged them, but she was too caught up in her own misery to do anything more. Later she saw them again at the house, where she and Carl received visitors. She moved through it all woodenly, shaking hands, forcing a smile she didn't feel.

Sam managed to steal a quick minute with her. "Annie, you look awful," he whispered. "Is there anything I can do?"

"It was all my fault, Sam," she said as tears ran down her cheeks. "I humiliated him in front of his friends and business associates. I don't know how I'll ever forgive myself." She turned and made her way up the stairs before he could say anything.

For two days she kept herself locked in her room, turning her nose up at the trays of food Vera brought up. The housekeeper was taking it hard too; it showed in the deepening lines of her face. On the third day, Annie listened silently in her father's library as his last will and testament was read. The realization that she was now a millionairess made no difference to her. She had no desire to take over running the various companies. The mere thought only added to her sense of panic and desperation. Fortunately, Eldon had called a doctor to the house early on, and Annie was given a light tranquilizer. She popped one in her mouth and slept the remainder of the day.

Sam received a full report on Annie's activities from his investigator friend, Will Smalls, a week later.

"She hasn't left the house since the funeral," the man said. "She takes zero calls."

"Is there any way to get to her?" Sam asked.

"Not unless you land a chopper or a hot-air balloon inside. They keep two guards at the front gate at all times. You probably know that from being there before. Nobody goes in or out without them saying so. Simple as that."

"There's got to be a way to get to her," Sam said, although he had no idea what it was.

Eldon stood in the Hartfords' library one evening and regarded Annie with a look of intense sadness and worry. "Hon, you have to snap out of this," he said, his tone authoritative, "or I'm going to insist you see someone."

Annie stared at the roaring fire in the fireplace. She was drowsy and ready for bed despite it being early. "Insist is a strong word, Eldon," she said flatly. "Perhaps you should rephrase that."

He knelt beside her chair. "I'm frightened for you, Annie," he said. "You can't stay holed up in this place forever. It's been a month now since the funeral. Look at you, you're skin and bones. How long are you going to ignore your friends? As sole heir to your father's estate, you have a responsibility to look after his holdings."

"I'm too tired."

"You're not still taking those tranquilizers the doctor gave you?"

She shook her head. "I only took one. Vera must've thrown the bottle away because I haven't seen it."

He sighed. "I'll take care of the most pressing business, Annie. At least for now."

She looked at him. "You will?"

He touched her cheek. "Why wouldn't I, honey? You know how I feel about you. Besides, you don't know anything about running a company, especially as many as your father owns. You were raised—"

"I know what I was raised to do, Eldon," she said. "To throw parties and look beautiful so I could snatch a man and have a slew of kids."

"Those rules no longer apply, sweetheart. Frankly, I'd like to see you at the helm of some of your father's companies."

She looked surprised. "You would?"

"Certainly. You could start small and work your way up. You know I'd do everything possible to help you."

"And why would you do that, Eldon?"

He didn't hesitate. "Because I love you, and I'm hoping there's a chance for us after all. That's all I'm asking for, Annie. A chance."

She yawned wide. "I don't love you, Eldon."

His jaw grew rigid. "Of course you don't. But you might surprise yourself one day and fall madly and hopelessly in love with me. In the meantime there's a lot of work to be done, and I can't very well go waltzing into your father's . . . or rather *your* companies without some sort of endorsement from you. We'd make a good team, Annie. I wish you'd reconsider marrying me."

Annie was having trouble holding her eyes open. The cup of coffee Eldon had poured for her had not given her the caffeine kick she'd needed. "So you're saying ours would be a marriage of convenience, and there would be no sex involved?"

Eldon was getting angry. It was obvious by the beet-red color in his face. "How many times has he called you, Annie?" he asked. "How many times has this Sam fellow so much as dropped you a line?" When she looked away, he went on. "Face it, hon, it was nothing more than a fling. Did he know what you were worth?"

She looked at him. "Go to hell." He had touched a sore spot. Sam hadn't bothered to contact her even once. In the beginning she'd been too devastated and filled with guilt to talk to him, but as the days wore on she'd longed to hear his voice, and know that he still cared.

"You're picking on the wrong guy. I'm on your side,

Annie. I've been here for you all along. What you had with him was fantasy; this is reality. You say you're tired of being treated like a mindless Southern belle? Then stop acting like one and take some responsibility for once in your life." He paused to catch his breath. "You can't just lie around feeling sorry for yourself while everything your father ever worked for goes down toilet."

Annie didn't realize she was crying until Eldon gently wiped a tear from her cheek.

"Bad news, Sam," the investigator said several days later. "She's going to marry the guy."

Sam sucked in his breath. He felt as though a tractor trailer had just landed on his chest. "No way."

"The wedding is going to be small out of respect for her father's recent death. It's to be held in the family home three days from now. They've already applied for a license."

"Dammit to hell!" Sam slammed his fist against the top of his desk. "Will, you've got to get me in there. I don't care how you do it, just do it."

Annie sat at the kitchen table in her bathrobe, sipping her second cup of coffee as she made a mental list of all she had to do before her wedding guests arrived that evening. She was still so very tired. It was as though the life had been sucked right out of her.

"Here, sweetie, have some of this crumb cake," Vera said. "You've got to eat something."

It was on the tip of her tongue to say she wasn't hungry, but one look at the housekeeper's worried face changed her mind. Annie pinched a piece of the cake off and put it into her mouth.

"That's my girl," Vera said. She sat there for a moment, fidgeting with her hands. "I've been needing to talk to you for some time, Annie. You've been so distraught that I was afraid to say anything, and I—" Her eyes teared. "I'm afraid I haven't been much better. But there's a few things I think you need to know before you go through with this wedding."

Annie met her gaze. "I'm listening."

Vera glanced around to make sure they were alone. "I know you've been blaming yourself for your father's death, but it wasn't your fault. Your father suffered heart problems for years. His heart attack was not a result of you walking out on your wedding as I suspect Eldon is leading you to believe."

Annie's eyes pleaded with her to be right. "Are you sure?"

"Mr. Hartford had been on nitroglycerin for years. Only a couple of people knew, but he forbade anyone to tell you."

Annie's eyes filled with tears. She was so weak with relief that her body trembled. "Oh, Vera. If only I'd known."

"Sweetie, I've been wanting to tell you since the funeral, but Eldon dared anyone to speak of it. Just as he—" She paused and lowered her eyes.

"As he what?" Annie asked. "Tell me, Vera."

Vera pursed her lips. "Well, it's obvious he thinks he owns the place," she said. "But he told me to make sure certain phone calls did not get through to you. And I was not to mention them. He threatened to fire me without my severance pay. I don't like that man, but I've felt too beaten down lately to stand up to him. I can't let you marry him without knowing what I know."

Annie's temper flared at the thought of Eldon threatening her beloved Vera. "He actually said he'd fire you?" When the housekeeper nodded, Annie shoved her cake away and crossed her arms. "What calls did he forbid you to let through to me. Were they regarding Daddy's companies?" She tried to be generous with Eldon, thinking he'd only been looking after her welfare. She definitely hadn't been herself these past six weeks. If there were business problems and he'd hoped to keep them from her, then she appreciated it, although she would not tolerate him mistreating Vera.

Vera raised her eyes to Annie's once more. "The calls I wasn't permitted to mention came from a Mr. Sam Ballard."

"Mr. Ballard phoned me?" she asked, holding her breath.

Vera blinked tears. "Five or six times a day, every day since the funeral. He even sent the police to the house, but Eldon was here at the time, and assured them you were okay, that you were just resting." She paused to catch her breath. "Another man, some kind of private investigator, has tried to get through the front gate, but he didn't make it in."

"Vera, you should have said something," Annie told her.

"I wanted to, but you weren't yourself. All you've done is sleep and cry. I've been so worried about you, but Eldon kept telling me you were coming around. You still sleep too much, in my opinion. It's time you were up and about."

Something nagged at Annie. "Vera, did you take that bottle of tranquilizers from my room?"

"I haven't seen any bottle of pills in your room, dear. Why do you ask?"

"You're right. I haven't been myself lately. I'm beginning to think Eldon has been slipping something in my tea or coffee. He's always here in the morning when I'm having my first cup, and he stops by at night for a cocktail."

Vera looked shocked. "But why would he do such a thing?"

Annie's eyes teared. "To keep me groggy and disoriented. So that I would depend on him more. And so I'd marry him," she added. She looked up. "I want you to inform the guards not to let Eldon on the premises no matter what. If he tries to get through, they are to call the police."

"Very well," Vera said. She went for the phone, but it rang just as she reached for it. "It's the security guard," she told Annie. "The florist is here."

"Already? They're not expected till this afternoon." She sighed. "Might as well let them in. We can always send the flowers to that nursing home not far from here." She glanced at her watch. "I need to get dressed. But first I'm calling Eldon to let him know the wedding is off. If he gives me grief, I'll threaten to press charges for keeping me doped up all this time. Funny he hasn't shown up this morning already. I suppose he wants me coherent for the wedding." She hurried toward the stairs.

Vera let the men inside a few minutes later. "I'll show you where to put things," she said, leading them toward the back of the house. "Let me know if you need something. I'll be in the kitchen."

Sam glanced around as he carried a basket of flowers to the massive living room at the back of the house. Will walked up beside him carrying a funeral wreath. "Why the hell did you get that?" he asked.

"Hey, I just hit every florist in town and picked up whatever was on sale."

"Hide it behind something, it looks awful."

"This is no time to get picky," the investigator said. "What are you going to do now?"

"I'm going to try to sneak upstairs and find Annie. You just keep bringing in flowers." Sam left him standing there and climbed the sweeping staircase to the top floor. He had no idea where Annie's bedroom was. He peeked inside several doors and found the rooms empty. The sound of a radio or tape playing instrumental music made him pause. He followed the music. He cracked the bedroom door so he could see inside, taking great caution. He didn't know if Annie would throw herself into his arms or throw something *at* him. He just didn't know her anymore. He didn't know if her grief had sent her over the edge, or if she'd been brainwashed or what.

But he was determined to find out, even if he had to resort to kidnapping her.

The sound of running water from the next room told him she was showering. He glanced around, snatched a patchwork quilt from a wooden stand and a scarf from the dresser. Very quietly, he opened the bathroom door and went in.

Annie couldn't see or hear a thing because the shampoo had gotten into her eyes and ears. But some sixth sense told her she wasn't alone in the bathroom. The thought that Eldon might be there startled her. She turned as the glass door swung open. She saw movement and opened her mouth to scream, but something was stuffed inside it. A quilt or bedspread was immediately thrown over her. Without a word, the man threw her over his shoulder and carried her out, pinning her arms to her side inside the quilt so she couldn't scream.

Will saw Sam coming down the stairs and motioned him to move faster. As Sam passed through the door and stepped into the truck, Will slammed the doors and hurried around to the driver's side. The guard motioned him through the gate, but he didn't have to be told twice. He sped down the road toward the highway.

It was all Sam could do to hold Annie still. It occurred to him suddenly that she might not be able to breathe, and he pulled the blanket off as fast as he could, at the same time yanking the scarf from her mouth. Eyes still closed, Annie opened her mouth to scream, but Sam stopped her by kissing her hard on the mouth. Her eyes popped open in surprise.

"Oh, Sam!" she cried, throwing her arms around him and kissing his face.

Sam glanced at Will, who was gazing at them over his shoulder. Sam made sure Annie was covered with the quilt. "See, I told you she was crazy about me." Suddenly Annie slapped him in the face so hard, he saw stars. "She has mood swings, by the way."

"Sam Ballard, what the hell do you mean sneaking into my bathroom and scaring me half to death? I thought you were a real kidnapper." She grabbed the scarf and tried to rub the soap out of her eyes and ears, then, seeing the quilt had slipped down to the swell of her breasts, she pulled it up indignantly. "Couldn't you have waited until I put on some clothes?"

Sam touched his jaw. "Babe, I didn't know if you'd come with me. I mean, you wouldn't accept my calls or letters."

"You wrote letters?"

"I wrote to you every day, but you never answered."

"Oh, Sam, I'm so sorry. I never received word of any calls or letters."

"And then when I heard you were going to marry Eldon—" He paused and frowned. "Dammit, Annie, every time I turn around you're about to be married to some other man. Has it ever occurred to you that I might make a damn good husband?"

"Oh, sweetie, I'd love to marry you."

"I don't know, Annie. You seem to accept every marriage proposal you get."

"Do you trust me, Sam?"

He met her gaze. He did trust her, despite everything. "Yes, of course I do."

"Then please give me a chance to explain the whole thing. But right now I'd like to borrow your car phone. My housekeeper will be worried sick."

Will passed a phone to the back and Annie called her house. A frantic Vera answered, and Annie assured her everything was okay. "I'll be in touch, Vera," she added before hanging up. "I just have one more call to make," she said. She called Eldon, who sounded as though he was just getting up. "Listen closely, Eldon," she said, her voice hard as stone. "First of all, I am not marrying you. Got it?" When he started to protest, she went on. "Shut up and listen to me. You stay away from my residence, you hear? The guards have been told to shoot you on sight. If you so much as come near the place, I'm calling the police to report that you've been drugging me. I may not be able to prove it, but your mother will never forgive you for creating such a scandal." Annie hung up and almost collapsed against Sam.

"Are you okay, Annie."

She nodded. "I just want to go home, and I want you to hold me until we get there."

Sam opened his mouth to Will, ready to give him instructions, then glanced down at Annie. "Where's home, babe?"

"With you, Sam. Wherever that might be."

FOURTEEN

It was a perfect day for a wedding; the sun was shining, the air was as crisp as freshly washed sheets on a clothesline. The fall leaves fluttered and spun about as a cold wind whipped through, bringing with it the smell of smoke from someone's chimney. The leaves scattered across a cracked sidewalk and crunched beneath the feet of those entering the little church.

Annie was dressed in a white wool-and-crepe suit with satin lapels, and Sam wore a navy suit. As they stood in the little church and exchanged vows, with their closest friends watching, Annie realized she'd never been happier. In the front row, Carl Yeager, the Hartfords' attorney, beamed proudly, having walked Annie down the aisle. The night before, Annie had asked him to see to the sale of her father's companies, as well as the family estate. She had no desire to be saddled with it any longer. She had no idea what she would do with the money; perhaps she'd buy cattle and she and Sam could be ranchers. She would keep the books, of course. And she would use a portion of the money to spruce up the town—a new theater, and boys' and girls' clubs for the kids. She wanted to give back some of the love her friends had shown her. Vera would not only get her severance pay, she would be set for life. Annie couldn't help but smile at her friends.

Lillian, who sat next to Carl, fluffed her hair and smoothed the wrinkles out of a dress that resembled one Annie remembered from the secondhand shop. Lillian had disguised it with lace, of course. Darla, wearing a short dress with bright tulips and matching hat, blew her nose loudly into a wad of tissue while Bo tried to calm her. Across the aisle, Kazue and Inge looked teary-eyed as well. And in the very front row, Vera and Sneddley, the chauffeur, gazed at Annie lovingly. Sneddley, who had seen to his prostate trouble, had made a point of putting his car keys in his pocket so Annie wouldn't take off again, but Annie had promised she had no intention of leaving this fiancé at the altar.

Annie turned back to Sam and gazed at him with all the love she had in her heart. After he'd kidnapped her that day, he'd taken her to his house, where he and Martha had seen to her care. They'd practically fed her round-the-clock, but Sam had made sure that she'd gotten plenty of exercise and fresh air as well. Sam had sent his investigator friend back to Atlanta to check out Annie's claims of being drugged, then he'd taken her to the doctor to make sure there were no lasting effects. She received a clean bill of health, but it was all she could do to keep him from going back to Atlanta personally and taking care of Eldon.

Finally, Annie was told to place the ring on Sam's

finger and repeat after the minister. Sam smiled at her tenderly as she said her vows. They had not shared a bed since her return, and the look in his eyes was full of promise. When it was his turn, Sam gently placed the ring on Annie's finger, and his gaze locked with hers while he promised to love and honor her.

Annie felt as though her heart would burst with love for the man.

". . . I now pronounce you husband and wife," the minister drawled. "You may kiss your bride."

Sam wasted no time pulling Annie into his arms. He kissed her deeply. When he raised his head, he was smiling. "I think I could get used to this."

"I'm counting on it, big guy," Annie said.

EPILOGUE

Sixteen Months Later

Annie had just finished her last appointment for the morning when she heard a ruckus outside her office. As she closed the ledger on her desk her fingers were already busy, undoing the buttons on her blouse. A knock at the door and Sam peeked in. One arm cradled a plump five-month-old, the other held a teddy bear and diaper bag. "Is the coast clear?"

Annie smiled at the sight of her handsome husband, struggling to get through the doorway with baby and paraphernalia. He was dressed in faded jeans and a blue work shirt, and the sheepskin vest she'd given him for his last birthday. He looked like the cattle rancher he was, and she adored him as much as she did the son that strongly resembled him.

"Bring Sammy Junior over here and I'll give him lunch," she said, pushing her high-back chair from the solid oak desk. Sam had given her his office once she'd received her associate's degree in accounting, and now it served as both office and nursery. Sam and Martha tended little Sammy when Annie had appointments, which she kept to a minimum because of the demands of motherhood; and she worked on her books while the baby napped or played.

Sam handed her the fuzzy-headed infant, and the baby automatically turned his head toward his mother. Once he'd found a breast, his mouth fastened onto a nipple, and he refused to let go. Annie was in the process of weaning him—he'd fussed when she'd introduced him to a bottle—but she still nursed him once a day because she enjoyed the closeness they shared. She loved being a wife and mother, and she was not ashamed to admit it to her single friends, who sometimes looked at her strangely when she brought out baby pictures and gushed over them.

Sam sat in front of Annie's desk and watched her nurse their son, his look one of pure adoration. He'd been thrilled when, after their wedding, she'd told him she was in a hurry to start a family. He'd enjoyed every day of her pregnancy, taking delight in watching her belly swell with his baby, holding her in his arms when she became weepy-eyed over something silly. They'd attended all the doctor's visits together, and Sam had held her hand and coached her through her labor. He was so damn happy, he didn't know what to do with himself. And he was proud of her. She'd worked hard to get her associate's degree in almost half the time it took most people.

"How's it going, little mama?" he asked Annie.

"Pretty good," she said, smiling at the man who took her breath away every time she looked at him. "I have a new account."

"Not bad," he said. "I hope you don't end up too busy to do my books."

"That's not going to happen, Mr. Ballard, and you know it. I've always got time for you."

"After all, I gave up my office so you'd have a place to work."

"Must I remind you that I completely renovated the attic and added windows so you could see the river? And that I furnished it to your liking?"

It was true, of course. Annie had hired men to knock out walls and restore the wood floors. The room was huge, with plenty of shelves for his law books, a desk and credenza, and several other pieces of furniture. It even had a TV and VCR, a stereo, and some of his workout equipment. Annie spoiled him rotten, and he knew it. They spoiled each other.

"I suppose it's an okay office," he said, "but I was sort of hoping to be compensated on a regular basis for my sacrifice."

"You've been compensated, pal. You have enough cattle to keep you busy until you're an old man."

He grinned. "That's true. When I said I wanted to ranch cattle, I wasn't exactly counting on a thousand head. I had planned to start small."

"I would have bought twice that, but I wanted to leave you some time on your hands in case anybody in town needed a good lawyer."

"The rate these critters are breeding I'm going to have to buy more land."

"So buy it. You know where the money is."

Sam's smile faded. "I can afford to buy the land, babe.

I've got money from the sale of my properties. I don't need my wife to take care of me."

Annie saw she'd touched his tender spot. Her husband could get cranky when it came to her inheritance. He didn't want people to think he'd married her for her money, and although he was more than appreciative when she did things for him—such as bring in all that cattle—it sometimes embarrassed him. "Sam, that's not what I meant. Everything I have is yours. I don't worry about what's yours or what's mine. I don't want you to worry about it either." She sighed. "Lord, some men would be glad to be married to a wealthy woman."

Sam stood and rounded the desk. He stroked his son's cheek. "I'm not one of them," he said. "I kinda liked you when you were a poor waitress, living in a garage apartment and riding a bicycle to work. That's the woman I fell in love with."

"I'm still that woman, and you know it. You just get a charge out of teasing me."

He pressed a kiss against her forehead. He did enjoy teasing her about being a millionaire, and true, he did sometimes get embarrassed over it, but he was proud as a peacock when she used her wealth to better the town. They lived a simple life, and Annie knew she would never have to earn a living if she didn't want to, but her job was important to her, even if it was only for a few hours a day. She had already told Sam she planned to go for her master's degree in accounting and her CPA, although she would hold off working full-time until Sammy was in school. Sam hoped Sammy would have brothers and sisters, but he would never push.

"I'm sorry," he said as Annie moved the baby to her

other nipple. He tried not to notice how wet and swollen the other one was from his son's suckling, but he could feel himself growing hard at the sight.

Annie looked up. "What are you sorry for, sweetheart?"

"Teasing you. You're right, I love to do it. I was hoping I could get you into a playful mood."

She arched one brow. "Playful?"

"Martha's gone to the grocery store. You know how long it takes her." He reached down and ran his finger around the wet nipple. It had already started to relax, but it contracted the minute he touched it.

Annie noticed Sammy Junior was already asleep. "I have to change the baby first."

"Already did it," Sam said proudly, remembering a time when changing his son's diaper was quite a challenge. "All you have to do is put him in his crib."

"Hmm. If I didn't know better, I'd think you planned this."

He kissed her softly on the lips. "Annie Ballard, let's get something straight. I planned to have you the first time I laid eyes on you."

"Oh, really?" Even now he could make her stomach flutter. "So, what do you plan to do with me now that you have me?"

Sam pulled her to a standing position. He arched against her so she could feel his hardness. "Put the baby to bed and I'll show you."

Annie started for the door, but he stopped her. She looked up and found his eyes filled with love and desire. "One thing I plan to do with you now that you're mine," he said softly, "is never let go."

THE EDITOR'S CORNER

With these, our last LOVESWEPTs, so many thanks are in order, it's impossible to know where to start. I feel a little like those people at awards ceremonies—afraid of leaving someone off the "thank you" list.

It goes without saying that we owe our biggest thanks to the authors whose creativity, talent, and dedication set LOVESWEPT apart. As readers, you've experienced firsthand the pleasure they brought through their extraordinary writing. . . . Love stories we'll never forget, by authors we'll always remember. Nine hundred and seventeen "keepers."

Our staff underwent a few changes over the years, but one thing remained the same—our commitment to the highest standards, to a tradition of innovation and quality. Thanks go out to those who had a hand in carrying on that tradition: Carolyn Nichols, Nita Taublib, Elizabeth Barrett, Beth de Guzman, Shauna Summers, Barbara Alpert, Beverly Leung, Wendy McCurdy, Cassie Goddard, Stephanie Kip, Wendy Chen, Kara Cesare, Gina Wachtel, Carrie Feron, Tom Kleh, and David Underwood.

Special thanks go to Joy Abella. Joy often said that being an editor for LOVESWEPT was her dream job and not many people got to realize their dreams. Thanks, Joy, for helping us realize how lucky we all were to have been a part of this remarkable project. ☺

Finally, thank you, the readers, for sharing your thoughts and opinions with us. Fifteen years of LOVESWEPTs was possible only because of your loyalty and faith. We hope you will continue to look for books by your favorite authors, whom you've come to know as friends, as they move on in their writing careers. I'm sure you'll agree they are destined for great things.

With warm wishes and the hope that romance will always be a part of your lives,

Susann Brailey

Susann Brailey

Senior Editor